MW01041906

SUNFLOWER

SUNFLOWER

by

Diane O. DesRochers

©2008 DIANE O. DESROCHERS

ISBN: 978-0-9814956-4-4

All rights reserved. Please do not participate in or encourage piracy of copyrighted materials in violation of the author's rights. Purchase only authorized editions.

This is a work of fiction. Names, characters, places, and incidents either are the product of the author's imagination or are used fictitiously, and any resemblance to actual persons, living or dead, businesses, companies, events, or locales is entirely coincidental.

This book or parts hereof, may not be reproduced, stored in or introduced into a retrieval system or transmitted in any form or by any means electronic, mechanical, photocopying, recording or otherwise. It may not be translated without prior written permission of both the copyright holder and the publisher of the book.

Fiction Publishing, Inc.
Ft. Pierce, Florida 34982
fictionpub@bellsouth.net

Dedicated to my beloved grandchildren
Jamie, Christopher, Jenny, Amanda, Chelsea,
Justin, Carter, Kaila, Cameron, Jordan

========

A special thanks to my family and friends, especially to Maureen and her third grade class who piloted the book in its infancy and offered many interesting comments.

I am forever grateful to Morningside Writers, Scripteasers and WordWeavers for their invaluable friendship and critique. Also, thanks to Marion Lonestar for her expertise and for making me an honorary member of her tribe.

Chapter 1

Village in Ruins

Blueberries, usually abundant near the swamp, were scarce this summer and it took a long time for Sunflower to fill her basket. When at last her container could hold no more berries, she started for home. Startled, she stopped and sniffed the air, catching the scent of smoke. But it wasn't the usual smell of the cooking fire.

What can it be, wondered this girl of ten summers. Clouds of smoke billowed from the direction of the village. The girl trembled. "Aiee, what is wrong?" Frightened, Sunflower raced for home but stopped when she heard the sound. She knew it wasn't thunder. *It sounds like the shooting stick!* As she sprang for the rocks and crouched behind a boulder her precious berries spilled from the basket. She started to pick them up but her sensible nature told her to wait. It felt like a nightmare to this terrified child as she stifled a scream and held very still. Her mind was filled with fear and dread of what was happening in her village.

The drought of the past few years was particularly trying for the Lenni Lenapé Indians. The corn, beans and squash they planted were withered and skimpy. Streams dried up and fear of the ever-encroaching white man was always there. So far, this village had been spared but marauding bandits destroyed several neighboring villages. Some families moved north in hope of finding a more plentiful land and the few remaining families were staying only until *Siquank,* the *Season of New Leaves*, when they too would migrate to join the Big Lakes People.

Sunflower asked her friend Grasshopper to pick berries with her.

"I cannot come today," was the answer, "I promised I would help Mama."

"I will share my filled basket with you then," said Sunflower as she skipped down the path and through the woods. When she came to the rocks near the stream, she carefully climbed over them and down through the thick brush searching for the delicious berries, inhaling the pungent dampness of the swamp.

"I'm glad I put bear grease on my arms and legs. The mosquitoes get stuck in the grease and cannot bite me," Sunflower said aloud to no one in particular.

Just the week before, the young girl had gathered and carefully wrapped partridge berries, moss and lichen in her apron. She arranged them in the cracked, but treasured clay bowl she'd found on a previous venture. With a covering of soft green moss on the bottom and the grayish lichen and red berries on top, it made a lovely present for her grandmother. Ohum adored the precious gift from Sunflower, the eldest of three children of her deceased daughter.

Flower that Blooms in the Sun, or Sunflower as she was more often called, was named for her sunny nature. When her mother died giving birth to twin boys it was Ohum who comforted Sunflower. And it was Ohum who nursed the children back to health when they were ill. She cared for the boys day after day and taught her granddaughter to sew and to cook. She also showed her where to find the special herbs, roots and bark in the forest, which she used for medicine.

As the Village Healer, Ohum was well respected by all. She even went to some of the white villages when they needed her curatives. Sunflower never left the compound but loved to follow her grandmother around their village as she cared for the sick or when searching for medicinal curatives in the forest. She also helped prepare herbal teas for a cough or a willow bark infusion to relieve pain. On more than one occasion the young girl watched with great concentration while Ohum set broken limbs, stitched the wound of a badly injured warrior or sometimes simply comforted a person who was upset.

Sunflower had many questions for her grandmother during their search in the woods and swamps. "What is this for, Ohum? Why do you use willow instead of pine or maple bark?" Inhaling the aroma of the leaves she'd picked, she said, "The teaberry leaf smells good. It tastes even better. What do you use it for?"

Ohum chuckled at all the questions and patiently answered her granddaughter's inquiries, explaining the various uses. Their relationship was warm and made closer by the child's interest in medicine.

Sunflower's brothers, Black Bear and Brown Beaver were now five years old. Because it was difficult to tell one from the other, the little pranksters liked to switch places and often fooled people, but Sunflower knew. There was just something about them that was different and she could always tell.

By the time she was ten, Sunflower was allowed to roam the woods by herself as long as she was within calling distance. She loved the freedom of being by herself, picking berries or searching for herbs, pretending she was a healer like her grandmother.

Long hunts frequently took the men away from the village. When they returned with their game, there was much work to do. Some of the women scraped the animal hides, removing the soft tissue while others prepared the meat for cooking and still other women stretched and dried the hide. Nothing was wasted and when they were finally through they celebrated with a feast, story telling, songs and dancing. It was an exciting time because the children were included in these festivities. Sunflower and her friends tried the dances and when they got mixed up, they giggled with laughter.

Sunflower was devoted to her family. When her father was home they took long walks and he told her wonderful stories. She treasured those times. Each day, she lovingly gave thanks to the Great Spirit in the Sky for the happiness bestowed upon her family and for giving them the land to use, care for and to share.

At last it was quiet. Sunflower waited a while longer, just to be sure, before cautiously creeping toward home. At the edge of the forest she hesitated, fearful of what she'd find but never expecting what she saw. Her village was in ruins! Wigwams had been ripped apart, some were smoldering and bodies lay everywhere. Sunflower shielded her face from the bloody gore. "Why, oh why?" she cried.

Sunflower recognized her friend who was bent over her dog as if trying to protect it. She ran to her. "Grasshopper! Are you...?" But the girl and her dog were both dead. There was blood, so much blood.

"Aieee! Father, Brothers, Ohum. Where are you?" she wailed.

5

Cooking pots and baskets were toppled over or strewn here and there. Where once was a well-organized village with lovely wigwams and stone-rimmed fire holes, it now looked like someone had dumped years of trash and set it afire. The frightened girl continued to thread her way through the rubble searching for her family but she found no one. It seemed that just a while ago she had everything and now all was lost.

Frantically, she tried to gather her belongings but when she reached under the remains of their once beautiful home for her sleeping robe it caught on something. She crawled under the rubble and there she found her beloved grandmother. At first, Sunflower thought the woman was dead. "Manito, Great Spirit in the Sky, please let her be alive," she sobbed. Ohum groaned. The girl carefully pulled the debris off her grandmother. The woman moaned again.

"Dear Ohum, there are so many dead. I don't understand what happened. I cannot find Father or my brothers. When I found you, I feared you too were dead."

Ohum managed a painful smile and lifted her hand that held a piece of the cracked clay bowl Sunflower had given her. It was broken into several pieces. It didn't matter now. Her grandmother was alive! All was not entirely lost.

Chapter 2

The Rescue

She wiped blood from Ohum's hair and her badly swollen face. Sunflower kept looking about, hoping her father had returned from his hunting expedition. At once she said, "Ohum, I will be back shortly." She pulled the bearskin sleeping robe around her grandmother and left to look around the village. "Surely, I will find my brothers or someone else alive. Ohum can't be the only survivor."

Weaving her way through the devastation, the Indian girl was sick to her stomach over the senseless slaughter and destruction. At last she found her brothers, but they too had been murdered.

Holding their lifeless bodies she wailed, "Black Bear, Brown Beaver, my beloved brothers. Who or why would anyone do this to you?" She sobbed for what seemed a very long time and when she thought there were no more tears, she prayed to the Great Manito to take their spirits to the heavens. With trembling hands she closed their eyes, something she'd seen Ohum do when a person died.

She wept over them again before returning to her grandmother.

"Ohum, they have killed my brothers. They have killed everyone. I don't know what to do. Please, tell me what to do," she sobbed.

"There, there, my precious child. It is hard to believe so many have been killed. I, too, weep for your dear brothers. They were born together and have died together. They join their dear mother now."

Sunflower's head reeled from the smoke and horror she'd encountered. "But why was our village destroyed? Why did they kill my brothers? Why did they hurt you? They didn't even take anything. They just destroyed it all. Why were they so cruel Ohum?"

The old woman didn't have answers for her distressed granddaughter. She simply reached out her hand and together they wept.

Later, Sunflower stood. She felt they should find a more secure shelter and that she had to take charge. "I have a plan, Grandmother. We may be the only ones alive but what if the bandits return? I fear we need to leave so that when Father returns from the hunt he will find us in the forest. If he doesn't come by the time you are healed perhaps we will go north to join with our people. I am sure he will know to find us there."

"You are right my child. We need to leave the village. You made a sensible plan." Ohum tried to get up but Sunflower motioned for her to stay where she was.

"Let me gather our things to take to the forest, then I will help you." Retrieving Ohum's medicine bag, she also found a supply of pemmican, the dried meat they'd prepared earlier in the month. Into her pocket, she put flint with which to start a fire, gathered another sleeping robe to keep away the chill of the night, and was busily assembling their things when the direction of her life changed once more.

Sunflower gasped and stifled a scream when she looked up into the strange face of a soldier. The tall white man with a trimmed beard startled the already frightened girl. He took her arm and spoke a strange language. His deep booming voice terrified her.

"Well," he said, "thank God, we've got a live one. Those bandits didn't kill 'em all." He spoke to two other soldiers as they too approached the girl. Sunflower slipped from the man's grip and ran to her grandmother's side, holding tight to the sleeping robe. Then, out of the corner of her eye she spied something. Suddenly, she dropped the robe and grabbed the broken handle of a hoe. With eyes flashing she stood her ground. She was prepared to defend Ohum and herself. Though her knees were shaky and she felt like crying, she stood firm not knowing what to expect but prepared to fight.

The tall man put his hand up and signaled for the others to stop. Then, using a soft voice, he said, "I didn't see this one." He knelt and spoke to the woman.

Ohum hesitated and then nodded. She looked at her granddaughter and in a weak voice said, "Precious child, these men will not harm us, they only want to help. I understand their language. They said they would take us to their healer."

Sunflower maintained her stance. "Ask if we can bury my brothers, first."

Ohum spoke to the tall man and he understood. "Show me where they are," said the tall soldier, signaling for the others to follow.

Sunflower tightened her grip on the hoe handle and led them through the rubble to where her brothers lay in a pool of blood. The men were shocked at the devastation. They found a shovel and dug in the earth.

"Just one hole for both. They belong together," Sunflower said.

The men seemed to understand. When finished, they lowered the youngsters into the hole. Suddenly, one man raced to the edge of the ruins and was sick to his stomach.

When they returned to Ohum, Sunflower allowed them to lift the woman onto their wagon. Quickly, she grabbed her things and climbed up next to her grandmother. Even though they helped to bury her brothers, she still didn't trust the men.

The soldiers again left to search through the shambles and finding no one else alive, buried the dead…old people, young people, babies…all were buried in shallow graves. When they returned, they looked grim. They said not a word, but quietly boarded the wagon and left the still smoldering village.

Sunflower didn't want to leave everything behind. She wanted to erase the last hours. She wished to make her brothers and her friend come back to life and she wanted to brush away the smoldering ashes from her home. Sunflower wanted her grandmother to be well and for her father to come home. But it was not to be. She took one last look at her village, bit her lip, and with tears streaming down her face silently cursed the bandits who'd destroyed the only home she'd ever known.

Sunflower was bewildered and deep in thought about their future, wondering if they'd return to their village when Ohum was well or if they'd leave everything behind to make the journey north. Her plans to stay in the forest had changed and she had to think of another idea. *Where will we stay? Will Ohum get well? What if she dies? What will I do then?* Sunflower looked at her grandmother who seemed to be sleeping and prayed to the Great Spirit to make her well.

Chapter 3

A Friend

"Ohum, this ride is so bumpy, it must be dreadful for you. Is there anything I can do for you?" Sunflower put her arm under her grandmother's head. Her own body ached from being jostled in the wagon as well. Ohum opened one eye. She shook her head and reached for Sunflower. They held each other for the remainder of the trip.

After bouncing over ruts and dusty terrain they arrived at Fort Joseph just as the sun was setting. They drove through the wooden gate. Log homes were erected along the pathway. There were other buildings too, which Sunflower was to learn were the general store, church and school.

As they drew near to the village many people gathered around. They stared at the newcomers. The women wore large bonnets and long skirts. Sunflower thought their pale faces looked sickly although they were nearly hidden from view. This young girl was used to seeing the proud women of her village in skin garments, decorated with quills and beads.

A soldier jumped off the wagon and sent a young boy for the doctor. Presently, a man wearing a white jacket and glasses appeared. The wagon came to a halt.

"What happened?" the man asked.

"Doc," explained the tall soldier, "we took a short cut through the valley and came upon a burning village. Those bandits have been at it again. These are the only survivors. The woman is hurt."

The doctor looked at Ohum and ordered the men to carefully take her from the wagon. Not understanding what they said, Sunflower was furious and bit the hand of the first man who touched her grandmother. He yelped. The others laughed. Then the doctor spoke soothingly to Sunflower and through hand gestures showed the frightened girl that he would not harm them but could help make the old woman well.

Then, and only then did Sunflower allow them to remove her beloved Ohum. She followed closely as they carried the now barely conscious woman into the log house and placed her on a narrow cot.

The medicine man looked at Ohum's wounds. He applied salve to her eye, stitched and bandaged the gash in her leg, then set her broken arm. The woman moaned. Instantly Sunflower was beside her. "She'll be fine," said the doctor. Although Sunflower didn't understand his words, she sensed

14

that all would be well. She stroked her grandmother's cheek.

Using a few words and hand signs, the medicine man told Sunflower that her grandmother should sleep and that Sunflower could stay with her. The exhausted girl dragged the sleeping robes from the corner where the men had tossed them and carefully draped one over Ohum. She snuggled into the other on the floor beside her.

Even though the day had been warm, Sunflower shivered. She was frightened, angry, and sad all at the same time. Her thoughts kept returning to the dreadful scene of the afternoon. In her mind she again saw her friend, Grasshopper. She remembered how her brothers were covered in blood, their beautiful home destroyed, the burning flames. It all seemed like a terrible nightmare. She prayed she would awaken and find that it was a dream after all. However, when she closed her eyes she immediately fell asleep and the next thing she knew the sun was shining.

Sunflower couldn't believe she had actually slept. "Ohum, are you awake?" she whispered. She pushed Ohum's hair back and noticed that the woman's eye was still swollen where the wigwam had collapsed on her. Her arm was in a splint and her leg was bandaged. Sunflower hugged the woman ever so gently. As Ohum smiled, Sunflower felt hopeful. "I know you will feel better soon," she reassured her grandmother.

The medicine man reappeared. He spoke and again Sunflower didn't understand his words. His manner was gentle, however, so she was not afraid. He inspected Ohum's wounds, put more salve on her eye, then motioned for Sunflower to follow him. In another room, a bowl of hot gruel and biscuits were on a tray. Although the aroma of the food was strange and tasted nothing like what they were accustomed to, it took away their stomach rumblings.

Distrustful of everyone at first, Sunflower continued to be cautious but the medicine man seemed extremely kind. During the next few days many people came to him and all were treated in the same caring manner. When the doctor pointed to an object and said the English word for it Sunflower retrieved the item, repeating the word as best she could. She enjoyed learning the strange language, but wanted her grandmother to hurry and get well so they could leave.

One day Sunflower walked into the office carrying clean bandages, but someone was there. Turning to leave, the doctor stopped her. "Wait, Sunflower," he said, "I want you to meet someone. This is Preacher Reed and his daughter, Melody."

He pointed to a girl who was nearly the same size as Sunflower. Her hair was blonde and she wore it in two braids just like the Indian girl. Her skin was pale and her turned-up nose displayed a sprinkling of freckles, but her blue eyes were as bright as the berries Sunflower had spilled on the rocks. She

16

smiled when the doctor introduced them and Sunflower knew they'd be friends.

When the preacher lifted his daughter from the table Sunflower covered her mouth with her hands. She was horrified. Bewildering thoughts went through her mind. Great Manito! The poor girl. Don't they feed her? Her legs are like twigs. No wonder she wears those iron sticks. Sunflower hesitated. She seems happy though and I can see that her father loves her. What happened to her?

Sunflower continued to puzzle over Melody long after she'd left. The doctor asked what was troubling her. Hesitantly, she told him her thoughts. With a chuckle he praised her for being observant but also cautioned her not to be quick to judge.

"Melody," he explained, "has been sick since she was a baby." He cradled his arms like he was holding a child. "Her muscles didn't develop as they should. Instead, they have become weaker until she can no longer walk without braces. But she is not in pain. She comes every week for her checkup."

Sunflower didn't understand all the doctor said but caught the gist of it. She liked the girl and looked forward to seeing her. After the doctor examined Melody, the girls visited while the men talked. Melody asked many questions of her new friend, some which Sunflower couldn't answer because she didn't comprehend the words. Often Melody didn't understand Sunflower. A strange sounding word or the way one girl pronounced a word often caused first one, then the other to giggle and soon they were both roaring with laughter.

Sunflower enjoyed being with Melody even though she was very different from her Indian playmates whom she missed. In her village, the children often played *gogo*, a game with sticks and a rock. Sometimes they walked through the woods or swam in a large pool at the end of the stream. The water was as clear as glass and cold as ice but they enjoyed it. At other times, they helped their families by gathering kindling wood for the fire. Older members carried the larger logs to the village. In winter they sat around the fire and decorated their moccasins or other garments with porcupine quills and beads or listened to the elders tell stories.

But Melody couldn't walk through the woods here, and there was no swimming hole nearby so they usually sat and talked. Sometimes Melody drew sketches of flowers or forest creatures, then pointed to the object and said the name for it. Sunflower gave her the Indian name and in no time each girl was learning the other's language.

Chapter 4

The Big House

Sunflower and Ohum were comfortable at the doctor's office, but knew that when Ohum was well they would leave to join their own people. One day Preacher Reed suggested that they live at his house. He said they could help Mrs. Reed with chores in exchange for food and a place to sleep. Mrs. Reed was a robust woman who walked with a cane. She didn't want the old woman living at her house. Sunflower steadfastly refused to leave her grandmother, so they compromised by letting Ohum stay in the shed attached to the house.

Sunflower was hesitant to live with the Reeds because she had hoped they could leave Fort Joseph to search for her father or other members of their tribe. But her grandmother was still weak and Sunflower knew they wouldn't be able to leave just yet, especially with the oncoming winter.

The Reed house was huge, consisting of many rooms. Some rooms were used for sleeping, one was where they ate and yet another was for cooking the food. Mrs. Reed taught Sunflower how to clean, make the beds, and do laundry in a large washtub. These things were new to Sunflower. Her beautiful wigwam consisted of one room. They slept on robes in a corner and cooked in the center. She was used to washing her clothes, as well as her body, in the stream near their village. It was all very simple and Sunflower liked it.

At first, Mrs. Reed seemed nice enough but she wore two faces. While others were around, she was sweet and kind, but when they were alone she scowled and beat Sunflower with her cane, all the while calling her wicked names. She said she hated that Sunflower was strong and healthy while her own precious child was sickly and weak.

Sunflower spoke to her grandmother about it. "Why is she cruel, Ohum? All white people are not that way. The doctor and preacher and Melody are not mean. Even the soldiers were not mean. Why does she hit me? Why does she hate me?"

"Precious Child of the Sun, it is difficult to understand some people. Most are kind, like the doctor and the preacher. I don't think they would hurt a person but Mrs. Reed seems very unhappy. Or maybe her mind is disturbed. I think it would be wise to treat her politely but try to stay as far away from her as you can."

So, while most of the time Sunflower felt sorry for the woman, there were times when her cane hurt, as did the woman's words.

20

"Sunflower, Sunflower. Good morning to you." Melody sang in her beautiful crystal clear voice.

"Hello, my new friend. What do you like to do today?" When Sunflower completed her chores, the girls often sat on a blanket in the shade of a huge elm tree where they talked or sometimes they visited with Ohum who told them the old stories. She had a way of telling them so that Melody could easily understand. These legends reminded Sunflower of her father whom she missed terribly and hoped that he would find them soon since they still couldn't leave.

Melody loved Ohum's stories too. Her favorite was about the Owl.

It seems that Ronie, who made everything, was busy creating the animals. Rabbit said to him, "I'd like long legs and ears like a deer and sharp fangs and claws like a panther."

"I will give you what you ask for," said Ronie, making Rabbit's ears very long.

Meanwhile, Owl who was still unformed, sat in a tree nearby and kept bothering Ronie. "Whoo, whoo, I want to be the most beautiful, the fastest, the most wonderful of all the birds. I want a long neck like Swan and beautiful red feathers like Cardinal, a long beak like

Egret, a beautiful crown of feathers like Heron, and..."

Exasperated, Ronie grumbled at Owl, "Just be quiet and wait your turn. Better still, close your eyes. You know no one is allowed to watch me work." Ronie was making Rabbit's hind legs long, just the way Rabbit wanted them.

"Whoo, whoo, nobody can forbid me to watch. Nobody can order me to close my eyes. I like watching and watch I will."

Now Ronie became very angry. As he grabbed Owl and pushed his head down into his body, Owl's eyes grew big with fright. Next, he formed Owl's ears until they were sticking up on both sides of his head.

"There, maybe this will teach you. Now you cannot crane your neck to watch things you should not see. And now you have big ears so you can listen when someone tells you what not to do. Your eyes are big, but not so big that you can watch me, because you'll be awake only at night and I work by day. Your feathers will not be red like Cardinal's but gray like mud. This is the punishment for your disobedience."

Owl flew off pouting, "Whoo, whoo, whoo."

*Ronie turned back to finish
Rabbit, but Rabbit was terrified and he
ran off half done.*

"What happened, what happened next?"
Melody asked excitedly.

"As a consequence, only Rabbit's hind legs are
long, so he has to hop about instead of running. And
because he was scared then, Rabbit continues to be
afraid of everything. As for Owl, he remains with big
eyes and a short neck. He sleeps during the day and
comes out only at night."

"I love that story," giggled Melody, "I can
picture Owl and Rabbit and even angry Ronie. Look.
I made a sketch of them." She held up her drawing.

Mrs. Reed called for Melody. When Sunflower
went to the door, the woman scowled. "Come out of
that shed immediately." As Sunflower helped Melody
down the steps, Mrs. Reed complained, "I don't want
you in there with that old woman. She smells bad and
I'm afraid that you will catch an illness from her."

Sunflower was confused. She couldn't
understand Mrs. Reed's reasoning. "I love Ohum's
fragrance of herbs and spices." But Mrs. Reed turned
away in a huff and went back into her house.

Sunflower had a cot in the same room as
Melody but when she was sure her friend was asleep,
the young Indian slipped from the cot to sleep on the
floor. It was more to her liking. She tried to bring the
bearskin sleeping robe to the room but Mrs. Reed
protested loudly.

It was difficult for Sunflower to adjust to the white man's ways. The food tasted peculiar and the clothing was awkward. Mrs. Reed insisted that Sunflower wear the clothing of the white woman. She gave the girl some of her castoff things but the blouse was large and the skirt was too long.

Ohum made a beaded belt for her granddaughter to wear and showed her how to shorten the skirt by hoisting it under the belt. However, the skirt was cumbersome and always in the way, especially when she scrubbed floors. How Sunflower hated wearing those clothes and longed for her soft doeskin skirt that Mrs. Reed had burned long ago.

Children went naked in the Lenni Lenapé village until they were eight or nine years old. Then girls dressed modestly in a tunic and a skirt that wrapped around the waist and fastened with a rawhide belt. The boys wore a loincloth and sometimes a shirt if the weather warranted it. Soft moccasins covered their feet.

Sunflower saved her moccasins, along with a quill headband but dared not keep these things in the house. Mrs. Reed would have destroyed them, so they were hidden in the corner of the shed where Ohum stayed. They were a reminder of a life of long ago, at least it seemed a long time ago to Sunflower. She still hoped that one day she and Ohum could return to their people. She looked over her treasures, while praying that her grandmother would get well. It seemed that Ohum was becoming weaker and she

24

slept for very long periods of time. Sunflower wanted to get the medicine man but Ohum said, "No." The girl was conflicted.

Mrs. Reed insisted that Sunflower attend church on Sunday mornings, but forbade her to sit in the front pew with them. She was told to sit at the rear of the church, alongside others who had dark colored skin.

Most of the people who lived in Fort Joseph gathered at the church. The congregation stood when a lady wearing a big hat played the organ. They sang from their hymnals. Sunflower could hear Melody's beautiful voice over the other singers. When the hymn ended, Preacher Reed stepped to the pulpit at the front of the church and spoke at great length to the people about God. He told them God was good. He said they should follow the example of God's son, Jesus, and they should be kind to all people. Even though Sunflower didn't understand all he was saying, she loved to hear him speak. His voice was loud; confident, yet comforting. When he finished, the congregation again sang.

Afterward, Preacher Reed and his wife stood just outside the doorway and greeted people as they left the service. Sunflower noticed how pleasant Mrs. Reed could be and wished that she were that way with her.

Chapter 5

School

"What is school?" Sunflower asked one day when Melody and her father were preparing to leave.

"It's a place where we learn to read and write."

"And what is...what ...read and write?"

This time the preacher explained, "In your culture, Sunflower, stories are passed down by your parents and grandparents. We preserve stories not just by telling them, but by putting the words in a book. This way the story never changes. It is always the same, from generation to generation."

"And the teacher helps us to recognize the words so we can read the stories whenever we want," said Melody. "Would you like to learn to read, Sunflower?"

Sunflower hesitated, not knowing what to say. She'd seen many books in the Reed house especially in the preacher's study. She liked to look at them with the strange writings and beautiful pictures. It would be good to learn to read the white man's language, she thought. "Yes!" she answered aloud.

"Well, come along then," said the preacher.

As they neared the log schoolhouse, Sunflower's hands felt clammy and her knees were shaky. She wasn't sure she wanted to go to school after all. There were other children entering the building and they stared at her. Sunflower hated that. In her village one never stared at another person. They were taught that it was rude.

Melody introduced her to the teacher who instructed the newcomer to sit in a vacant seat. Then she spoke. "Boys and girls. We have a new student. Her name is Sunflower."

A tall boy with buck teeth and red hair stood up and snickered, "What's yer last name, Injun?" The children giggled.

Sunflower was embarrassed and wanted to run from the building but only slipped further down in her seat.

The teacher read to the class, then wrote on a slate board. The children recited in unison what she had written. Sunflower listened. Then the teacher asked Sunflower how old she was.

"Ten summers and seven moons," Sunflower answered proudly.

The children roared. They thought it was funny.

"Settle down class," said the teacher. "Now I have a question for you. How many summers in a year?"

A girl with long curly hair raised her hand. "Just one summer in a year," she answered.

"And how many moons in a month?" asked the teacher.

This time a boy stood up and loudly exclaimed, "One moon in a month is usual, ma'am."

"Both of you are absolutely correct," she said. "Now, if there is one summer in a year and one moon in a month, how old is Sunflower?"

"I know, I know!" said the first girl. "She is ten years and seven months old."

"Very good. Sunflower has told us that she is ten summers and seven moons. That is the same as ten years and seven months. Now, just because someone answers in a different manner doesn't mean that they are wrong. As you go through life you will find that people speak many different languages and it would be to your advantage to try to understand, rather than ridiculing. Think about that. Class dismissed."

The children raced for the door. Sunflower wanted to hug the teacher for making her feel welcome but smiled shyly instead.

School was a challenge for Sunflower. More than once she wanted to stay home but Melody convinced her that she was doing well. It was difficult at first for her to explain herself in English words even when she could pronounce them correctly. One day the teacher told the children that their assignment was to talk about their grandparents, where they came from and what they did. She said she would call on them one by one the following week.

Melody was excited. She questioned her parents to be sure she had her facts straight and was the first to be called upon. She struggled to the front of the classroom. It was hard for Melody to stand so the teacher placed a chair facing the class for her. Melody sat, then told the other students, "My mother came from Staffordshire, England. She sailed to America on a big ship with her parents when she was young. She doesn't remember much about the trip but she inherited a beautiful set of china that was packed and shipped with the family. We use these dishes on special occasions like Thanksgiving and Christmas. This reminds me where my ancestors came from."

Another child spoke with a bit of a brogue. She and her family had come from Ireland, she said, and now lived on a farm where they grew potatoes.

Some children said their parents and grandparents had always lived here.

When it was Sunflower's turn, she was nervous. After taking a deep breath, she proudly spoke. "My ... ancestors ... are Lenni Lenapé of the Algonquian Tribe. They come from a place named after Lord De La War. Many use that name, but we ... we like Lenni Lenapé. It means original people. We are a peaceful and peace-loving people." Sunflower's hands were shaky. She clenched and unclenched them.

The teacher asked Sunflower to continue. "Tell us about your family," she said.

"My grandfather ... he have garden. No weeds. Straight rows. Corn up high..." Sunflower raised her

30

arm above her head to indicate how tall the corn stalks were. "Squashes were very big. He had secret. Grandfather loved to fish. Grandmother cook fish. We eat fish. Then Grandfather bury heads and bones of fish in garden. He make deep hole, put in leaves and pine needles, then bones. Much time pass. Bones dry. He pounded into... powder and spread around plants. That his big secret." Sunflower finally let out her breath and no longer felt nervous.

One child asked, "Where are your parents? Do you have sisters and brothers?"

"My mama... she die when twin brothers come. My father is...was...a hunter. My grandmother is Village Healer. We grow corn, beans, squash, or we did...then village in ruins."

The children were fascinated by her story and encouraged her to tell them more. So she told how their village was devastated and how the soldiers brought her to Fort Joseph.

"Were you scared?" asked a student.

"I was scared. I was angry too. I did not want to leave village. I did not want soldiers to take us without...permission. My Ohum was hurt. We did not have...a pick..."

The teacher helped by explaining that pick meant, a choice. They didn't have a choice.

Suddenly Sunflower didn't want to talk any more. She was exhausted having to tell her story and reliving the trauma and went back to her desk.

"Thank you," said the teacher and called on another student.

31

Melody smiled and whispered, "That was very good."

"Thank you." Sunflower mouthed. The children got used to the unusual way the Indian girl described things and she was often asked about her culture. They were thrilled when she showed how her people made baskets woven with swamp grasses that would actually hold water.

They asked about her home, her family and her friends and were saddened when Sunflower told them that only she and her grandmother had survived the day their village was destroyed and that everyone else, including her two brothers and her best friend had been killed.

Sunflower kept busy practicing her schoolwork, helping in the Reed house and spending time with her beloved grandmother. She decided she liked school. She excelled in arithmetic, had some difficulty at first in mastering the writing, but eventually learned that as well.

The friendship between Melody and Sunflower developed as they studied their reading and writing and learned more about one another.

Chapter 6

Ohum

Time passed quickly as Sunflower learned many new words and ways. But she continued to be troubled that although her grandmother's injuries had healed in the past two years, there was an inner wound that the old woman couldn't seem to shake. Ohum never ventured far from the shed and her stories, usually joyful, now contained sadness. Once strong and robust, she was now thin and bony.

Sunflower searched the woods for nuts and berries as a treat for her grandmother but even that didn't cheer the woman. She could sense Ohum's life slowly ebbing. One day the young girl ran to the medicine man.

"Please come," she pleaded, "my grandmother, she is not well."

The doctor was about to close his office and already had his leather bag in hand. He followed Sunflower and was surprised when she led him to the shed at the rear of the house. He muttered to himself when he saw the shabby room where Ohum lived. He listened to the woman's heartbeat and felt her pulse.

"How long has she been like this?" he asked.

Is he annoyed with me? Perhaps I should not have brought him here. I have never seen such darkness in his face. It frightens me. "Ohum not strong since we were captured," she said. "She not me want to bother you. I worry. Ohum weak. I know not what do."

The doctor patted Sunflower's arm. "You did the right thing, dear girl." He reached into his leather bag, removed a small bottle and poured some of the brown liquid onto a spoon for the sick woman. "I'm afraid your grandmother is gravely ill," he said sadly. "She is no longer young and cannot easily shake this illness."

Sunflower could only nod in reply. She knew. Her heart ached, realizing that Ohum's spirit would soon leave. Kneeling at her bedside, Sunflower stayed with her grandmother for a long while, comforting her and reminding her just how much she was loved.

Ohum lay quietly, occasionally sipping water. One day she asked to have her head propped. "I need to talk to you," she began. "My child, you grow more like your mother each day. She was very beautiful. And she, like you, was a kind person. Your father loved her very much. His heart broke when her spirit left."

34

Sunflower took her grandmother's hand. "Ohum, I don't think Father knows to look for us here. How will he find us?"

"Granddaughter, Flower that Blooms in the Sun. I love you more than life itself and would keep from hurting you. I have not told you this, but just before bandits destroyed our village, the men returned from the hunt. Although I did not see your father, I fear he may have been killed, along with the others."

Sunflower had hoped that her father would somehow find them. Now sadness enveloped her whole being as Ohum spoke. Words gave way to the fear that was in her heart... that she would never see him again. Together, they wept.

Later, when Ohum asked for the medicine bag she uttered, "My wish was that one day we would return to our people. But now I am old and weaken with each sunrise. It is unlikely that I can leave, but one day you must. This, my child, is important. You must join our people in the north."

As Sunflower removed the items one by one from the medicine bag, Ohum reminded her once again of the name of each herb or piece of bark or root, what it was used for and where to find it in the forest. She spoke at length about many things, most especially about survival in the forest. She knew that one day soon her granddaughter would need this knowledge.

"Be proud of your heritage, my child," she said. "Learn new ways but never forget the old laws of the tribe. Both are profound lessons. When you rejoin our people in the north, you can bring to them the things you have learned here. They, too, should know that to have peace among all people they need to understand them. Knowledge is the key, Sunflower."

Two nights later Ohum went into a deep sleep never to awaken. Sunflower lost her precious grandmother and learned her father was likely dead as well. A flood of tears ran down the heartbroken girl's face as she cried, not only for the loss of her beloved grandmother, but for the loss of her father and the happy life she once had.

Preacher Reed insisted they have a funeral for Ohum and ordered a pine coffin for her. Some women from the church prepared her body for burial. Sunflower went to the shed where her grandmother stayed. She wanted to put something into the coffin. She picked up the medicine bag but had second thoughts. *Ohum wanted me to use the skills she taught me. I must keep the bag.* She searched the small room and there beside the old woman's bed was the shard from the clay bowl. *I will send this with her.* She wrapped the piece of pottery in a square of suede and tied it with a strip of rawhide.

She approached the preacher. "Will you put in box with my grandmother? It meant much to her." The man took the small package and placed it in the coffin.

Besides the preacher, Mrs. Reed and Melody, only the doctor and the kitchen help, Henry and

Stella were mourners. As they gathered in the cemetery Preacher Reed said some words over the grave. Then Melody sang a hymn.

> *Lord, I know you know me*
> *More than others see*
> *My heart is yours*
> *Forever more*
> *Lord, I know you know me*

Sunflower wept. The words and music touched her heart. Her grandmother loved to hear Melody sing. Perhaps she was listening even now.

The doctor moved next to the Indian girl and put his arm around her shoulders. "I am so sorry for your loss, dear girl," he said. "Your grandmother was a kind woman and she taught you well. Although you suffer now, know that Ohum is no longer in pain."

The sad girl mouthed her thanks as she brushed away a tear.

Stella and Henry hugged the young girl. They too had tears in their eyes. Melody, sitting in her chair beside her dear friend, squeezed Sunflower's hand. Choking back the lump in her throat, Sunflower said, "I happy you sing. I know Ohum loved it." Melody smiled as her father led them back to the house.

Sunflower's sorrow seemed unbearable after her grandmother's death. Many times she'd dash to the shed to tell Ohum of her school day before she remembered that she was no longer there. She missed her terribly. There were things that she could share

37

only with her grandmother, things she couldn't tell Melody, especially about Mrs. Reed's cruelty.

Ohum had told her granddaughter that she'd be gone from her body but would remain with her in spirit. As she lay dying she said, "Whenever you see the Red Bird, know that I am there." Sunflower didn't understand but Ohum told her it would be revealed to her at a later time. Melody tried to console her. They had become close friends and the passing of Ohum saddened her, too. She especially would miss her wonderful stories.

Chapter 7

The River

Over the next few years, Melody's legs became weaker until she was unable to walk, even with braces. One day she called out, "My friend, look what Father had made for me. Watch. It feels like I am running."

Sunflower ran to her and examined a chair with wheels. "It wonderful is. I like it."

"It is wonderful," exclaimed Melody. "You can help me by pushing it."

Sunflower pushed her friend to and from school and everywhere in between. The chair enabled the girls to get around more quickly but Melody wanted to go faster.

"Whoa, I not a horse, my friend."

Melody laughed. "Watch me!" She was very daring and pushed on the wheels.

"Be careful. You might over tip."

"Ha! It won't tip over. I'll race you."

"No, please! I scared when you do that."

The girl stopped. "Okay, let's go down to the river today."

"Okay, but I push you," said Sunflower.

Down the road and around the bend they went until they came to the river where a barge was being poled downstream. Melody waved at the men on the barge, then pushed on the chair wheels herself to follow the barge. Faster and faster the chair sped down the embankment toward the water. Sunflower chased after her. She reached out but couldn't catch the elusive chair. Down, down it sped into the water where it bumped onto a big rock, catapulting Melody into the river. Sunflower plunged into the river after her. Her long dress weighed her down and it was difficult to move through the water but she dove under. The water was murky and she couldn't see well. When she came up for air she saw Melody's head bob up and was finally able to grab hold of her, just as her friend swallowed another gulp of water.

Fighting a feeling of panic, Sunflower managed to hold Melody's head above the water but the strong current pulled them out to the middle of the river.

"Help! Help!" They called. The pole man on the barge saw the girls, seized a life preserver and jumped into the water. A strong swimmer, he easily reached the girls. He threw the rope to Sunflower who grabbed hold of the rope while still thrashing. The man held Melody and put the life preserver over her head. Then he tugged on the rope and pulled

Sunflower closer to him. "Hold on!" he said as they made their way to shore.

Melody, although coughing and crying, was not injured. Sunflower was scared, especially when she looked up and saw the preacher pacing back and forth on shore.

Oh no, will he be angry at me for not watching Melody more carefully? She is soaking wet and may get chilled.

Preacher Reed's only concern was for his daughter's safety. He ran to the boatman who carried the sodden girl from the water. Reaching out, the preacher clutched his beloved child to his chest and moaned a brief prayer of thanksgiving. He profusely thanked the boatman over and over. When a bystander told him of the Indian girl's bravery and daring in trying to rescue Melody, he looked down and smiled his thanks to Sunflower before carrying his daughter home.

Another person fished the chair from the water where it had lodged against a boulder. The front wheels were bent. "I think it can be repaired," he said.

After the river incident both girls were much more cautious. "I'm sorry, Sunflower. I didn't think it would go so fast. I was scared to death when I fell into the water. I can't swim you know. You saved my life."

"I scared too when I could not catch you. I did not save your life, man on barge did."

Melody smiled. "I think you saved my life and I promise you can do the pushing from now on."

"I keep you to that promise, my friend."

Mrs. Reed was grateful her daughter was not hurt, only wet. She gave Sunflower one of her hateful looks, and later when they were alone, accused Sunflower of deliberately trying to drown her daughter.

"Aieee, how can I convince you I tell truth," cried Sunflower. "Melody is my friend. I not harm her." But Mrs. Reed continued to badger her relentlessly. The Indian girl gave up trying to explain.

Soon summer was upon them and the days grew hotter and hotter. The heat seemed to bother Melody so on one particularly hot and humid afternoon, Sunflower said, "I know what we do today."

"It is too hot to do anything," Melody moaned.

"Wait. This be nice, you see," she said spreading a blanket over a small bench Henry had made for the girls under the elm tree. She then filled a large washtub with cool water. Helping Melody to the bench, Sunflower removed her shoes and stockings and they both put their feet into the tub. Before long, they were having a wonderful time laughing and splashing.

Mrs. Reed came outside to see what the laughter was all about. When she saw Melody with her bare feet draped over the edge of the tub and her dress splattered with water, she was furious.

"What are you doing?" she screamed. "Get my precious daughter out of that water." She strode back into the house and sent one of the servants out with a towel to dry Melody and bring her into the house.

Sunflower emptied the tub, folded the blanket and picked up her friend's shoes and stockings. Mrs. Reed came out again, looked around to be sure no one was close by and beat Sunflower about her shoulders and back with her cane all the while screaming at her, accusing the Indian girl of trying to harm her daughter.

Sunflower raced to the edge of the woods and poured her heart out to her grandmother's spirit. "Ohum, why did you have to die? I don't know what to do. I was only trying to make Melody more comfortable. You know I would never hurt anyone, especially my friend. Why, oh why is Mrs. Reed so cruel?"

No answers were forthcoming, but the girl felt better after releasing her sorrows. She tried especially hard to do her chores without confrontation with the cruel woman.

Chapter 8

The Holidays

Surrounded by shades of scarlet, orange and gold hues, the people gathered pumpkins and squash from the frost-killed gardens and stored them in the cellars. The men hunted wild turkey, pheasant and deer while the women made pies and puddings in preparation for Thanksgiving. This was a happy time when families shared their abundant crops and celebrated with a great feast.

Sunflower polished Mrs. Reed's silver candlesticks until they gleamed. They were expecting many guests. Several people helped with the cooking and baking but Sunflower did all the cleaning. At last the house shone from top to bottom and the dining room table was set with the precious bone china that came from across the ocean. The aroma of roasted turkey, venison, and pies wafted up the stairs where Melody and Sunflower were dressing.

"I'm so hungry my stomach is growling," said Melody.

Sunflower laughed, "I think my stomach made that noise. We both hungry."

Grinning, Melody reached for the bell pull. Soon her father came to help his daughter downstairs.

"You girls look lovely," he said as he entered the room. He picked up his daughter and carried her down the great staircase. "Come along, Sunflower."

She followed but instead of entering the dining room with Melody and the guests, Sunflower made her way to the kitchen. She ate with Stella and her husband, Henry. Stella, a happy person besides being a wonderful cook always had a smile and a kind word for Sunflower. The young Indian girl felt at home and relaxed with them.

Mrs. Reed had been especially cruel again this morning and Sunflower ached from the beatings. *I must leave. One day soon I will.* She wondered if she should say something to Stella about Mrs. Reed but quickly changed her mind. *It is embarrassing and Stella might think ill of me. I will put it out of my mind for now.* She picked up her fork and tasted the delicious food.

Stella and Henry kept up a lively conversation. Henry asked Sunflower if she preferred the dark meat of the drumstick or white breast meat.

"Drumstick?"

"That's what we call the turkey leg. After you eat the meat, it looks like a stick used to beat a drum."

Sunflower laughed. "I like the white meat, but I love pumpkin pie most best. We not have pies in our village."

When dinner was over, she helped Stella with the dishes while Henry cleared the dining room.

Later, the *Month of the Falling Leaves* gave way to the *Month of First Snow* blanketing the ground with a covering of white. When the girls awoke, their eyes welcomed the beautiful scene. The weight of the snow bent pine branches to the ground. Everything had a pristine appearance, as though newly washed. The girls were disappointed though because now they couldn't take the chair with wheels. That day they sat and read by the fireplace but on the following day, Melody's father told them he had a surprise and showed them a sled they could use instead.

"Thank you, Father."

"I am exciting, Melody. Now we can go in the woods. I show you the different trees.

Melody had to chuckle to herself the way Sunflower sometimes expressed herself. She spoke the language well but sometimes mixed things up. "Yes, you are exciting and I am excited about going into the woods."

They bundled up against the cold and Melody was wrapped in a heavy wool quilt as she sat on the sled. Sunflower pulled hard to get the sled going, but after a while it glided over the crusted snow. It was quiet in the woods and reminded Sunflower of her previous life. She pointed out the different trees as well as footprints of various animals in the snow.

"What kind of animal made these marks?" asked Melody pointing to the ground.

"You silly! It is from snow melting on branches, then drop to ground." She laughed. "They do look like footprints though."

While in the forest, Melody tried to sketch but it was difficult to do so with mittened hands. Sunflower loved to watch as her friend captured the likeness of the trees and animals. When they got home, they sat by the warm fire while Melody copied her sketches onto a canvas.

"I can't paint any longer, Sunflower. Let's make necklaces with the pretty beads we bought at the general store."

"We can use the pumpkin seeds we colored too," said Sunflower, putting away the paints and retrieving the beads and beautifully dyed seeds.

"I'm having trouble threading the needle, do you think you can try it?"

Sunflower wet her finger, then pulled the fine cording through her pinched fingers, making a point that slid into the eye of the needle. "Here. Hope I can do for me too."

The girls threaded a seed onto the needle, pulled it through and onto the string. First a red one, next a yellow one, then a pretty blue glass bead. Next another yellow seed, then a red one.

"Do you think it looks pretty?" asked Melody.

48

"I do," said Sunflower. She used other colors and a completely different pattern emerged. When they had strung enough seeds and beads for a necklace, they secured them by tying a small double knot in the end. The excess thread was clipped off. They made matching bracelets too. "I'm making one for my mother, do you think she will like it?" asked Melody.

"Yes, I think," answered Sunflower. "This for Stella. I like her much. She always do nice things for me."

Caught up in the excitement of the coming holiday, they worked on their gifts to each other. Sunflower made a basket and Melody made a painting but they couldn't wait until Christmas so gave each other their gifts just as soon as they were completed.

Melody thought the basket was the perfect container for her paints. She hugged Sunflower, and then presented her gift. It was rolled and tied with a red ribbon. Sunflower carefully unrolled the gift. Her eyes filled with tears when she saw the painting, made especially for her. It was a red fox with a beautiful tail, peering out from a hollow tree. *Wallow.* Melody called it a fox. Sunflower loved it and would treasure it always. She hugged Melody before carefully rolling the painting up. She retied it just the way it was presented to her by her good friend.

One day Henry brought a large fir tree into the house and set it up in a corner of the parlor where guests were entertained.

"Why you bring tree into house?" asked Sunflower.

"Just wait and you will see, Sunflower. It is our Christmas tree. You will love it and it will be so beautiful. You can even help decorate it," said Melody, finishing her paper chain of red and green. Both girls helped to decorate the tree with handcrafted decorations.

Stella and Henry put ornaments on the highest branches while the girls adorned the middle and lower branches.

"It is beautiful," said Sunflower. "It brings my eyes to tears." She had never seen a Christmas tree before. It seemed to transform the house. It also seemed to transform its occupants as certainly Mrs. Reed acted differently. There was much laughter and a good feeling with the Spirit of Christmas, along with the hustle and bustle of friends stopping by.

The girls wrapped the gifts they had made and put them in a neat pile under the tree. "I'm so excited," exclaimed Melody. "I can't wait until Christmas morning."

Sunflower reflected on her life with Melody and the Reeds. It was difficult, especially now that Ohum was gone. I would stay if Mrs. Reed were not so cruel. I don't know why she is nice to others but is very mean to me. She carries a cane. Is it to beat me or does she need it to walk? Does she have the same illness as her daughter? Sunflower stopped. *I must stop. I am as cruel as Mrs. Reed with my words. I don't like me when I think like her.*

Sunflower tried being kinder to Mrs. Reed in thought and in deed. It didn't work though. As soon as the Christmas season was over, Mrs. Reed was as cruel as ever. In fact, she was getting worse and even raised her voice in front of Stella at times. Sunflower still didn't say anything although she was tempted to ask Stella what she could do to stop the woman. She remembered that her grandmother wanted her to find her tribe members.

I will seek them when winter is gone, she thought.

That winter was especially harsh, frequently snowing or sometimes sleeting, making it difficult to get out of the house. On stormy days when they weren't able to go to school, time dragged on. The girls did their best to keep occupied with crafts and stories, but they were often bored and longed for warmer weather.

Chapter 9

Spring

Spring finally came and with it a gradual warming. Rain, at first a welcome relief from snow and sleet that washed away the last traces of winter, now continued for days until the streets were thick with mud. Wagons left great ruts in the road. Everything looked and felt dirty. Merchants placed boards near the entrance to their shops, which helped somewhat, but the hems of the ladies' skirts were laden with the wet earth.

Sunflower longed for her cedar bark poncho instead of the heavy canvas tarp that Mrs. Reed made her wear. There was so much mud and the Indian girl was constantly brushing it from her shoes and off the wheels of Melody's chair, as well as having to sweep it from the doorway.

"Will the rain stop ever?" she complained.

In time, it did stop and just as trees that were bare all winter were now swollen with buds ready to blossom, so was Sunflower. She had grown taller and her ankles showed below her skirt. And she could barely button her blouse.

"You ugly girl. You're much too big for the dress you're wearing. Today we'll go to the yard goods store," announced Mrs. Reed. "We have to make you a larger dress."

Mrs. Reed is angry with me again. I didn't grow on purpose. I really am not so big like she says. I do not think I am ugly. Perhaps to her I am. I have grown. I am becoming a woman.

Melody accompanied them to the store. There was a large selection of fabric from which to choose. The girls found many pretty patterns.

"I love the one with pink flowers," said Melody.

"My best one is red with lines."

"The lines are called stripes," said Melody with a chuckle.

"Stripes," she giggled.

Mrs. Reed paid no attention to the girls and instead selected a dull brown, gray and black print with a touch of mustard yellow.

Why did we come with her? She chose the ugliest fabric in the store. I hate it. I want to rip it to shreds. Of course, I won't. There were many lovely fabrics, in beautiful colors and fine patterns but this, besides being ugly, is rough, not smooth like the leather garments I used to wear. I wish I had my soft doeskin skirt and moccasins. I saved Ohum's. They may fit me, now that I am so big.

Sunflower straightened up and with determination decided she would wear the moccasins. *They will be more comfortable than shoes. At least my feet will be free, even if I am not.* Sunflower felt rebellious. No one seemed to notice she wasn't wearing the heavy shoes and she continued to wear her grandmother's moccasins.

On the way home from school one day, there was much commotion on the pathway. When Sunflower and Melody arrived, children were crowded around a large bird on the ground. It was fluttering, trying to fly, but it couldn't. Black with white under its wings, its bill was large and its feet and legs were yellow.

When Sunflower saw it her heart leaped. "An eaglet! What happen to it?" She looked around. No one answered, but one of the boys had a slingshot hidden behind his back. The Indian girl set the brake on Melody's chair and walked slowly to the bird, murmuring in a soft voice. "I not hurt you." She knelt beside the bird and saw that its wing was folded over. Using her apron to cover the bird's head, she carefully picked it up and tucked it under her arm.

"What are you going to do with it?"

"How will you get it home?"

There were many questions. Sunflower didn't have the answers but she knew she had to help the bird or it would die. She ignored the other children and spoke to Melody who was waiting in her chair.

"Can you hold him?"

"I think so. I'll be careful. Ooh, look, it has long toenails."

"Watch it. Talons are sharp," said Sunflower as she placed the injured bird on her friend's lap. Melody put her arms around it. When bird tried to move Sunflower murmured to it again. "Hold him tight. Sing to him." Then she pushed the wheelchair home with her friend and the bird without further incident. The other children scattered.

When they got to the yard, Sunflower said to Melody. "Keep hold on while I find something to put in."

"It seems calm right now. I'll hold him."

"Don't take cover off." She entered the shed where Ohum used to live and found a large crate with a top. She set it near the door and to Melody she said, "I push you close to the doorway and take bird. You can see, but I must warn you, if it gets away from me you will need to duck. I don't want you to get hurt."

Sunflower checked the crate again, then removed the wrapped bundle from Melody's lap. The bird struggled but the girl held on and carefully set it in the crate. She left the apron over its head until she had the top of the crate in her hand. "Oh my, this will not work."

"Why? I think it would be safe."

"But how can we feed it? How will it get air? We need an open top." Sunflower looked around but found nothing she could use.

"What about wire? I think Henry has a roll of it in the chicken coop."

"Yes. Wait here, I hurry." Sunflower put the top on the crate temporarily and raced to the house. She found Stella in the kitchen. "Stella, I can ask a question?"

"Of course, dear. I just baked cookies, would you like one? What is it?"

"We found a bird. We want to put it in cage. Melody thinks you have wire we can use for top of cage."

"Why don't you put the bird in the chicken coop?"

"We could, but you don't you want it there. It is a young eagle. It is injured."

"My goodness, I'll get my husband. We'll meet you in the shed. He'll know what to do." In no time the couple headed back to the girls. Henry had a hammer, nails, a roll of wire and an armload of straw. Stella carried a container of cracked corn and a bowl of water for the bird.

"Isn't it just like Stella to think of food? She's always feeding someone or something," said Melody with a chuckle.

They made a top for the cage with the wire. Then Henry checked the bird's wing and agreed that it was broken. Sunflower found a sturdy stick. "Can we use this for...a... I don't know what you call it."

"A splint?" Henry felt the stick. "Yes, I think it'll work. We can attach it with twine." Leaving the apron over the head of the bird kept it calm while they applied the splint. When they were finished, they put the wire cover on the cage and gently removed the apron.

The bird shook its head and tried to flap its wings but there wasn't room in the small cage. Indignant, it let out a loud squawk. "*Kak, kak, kak*" It scared the group at first, but then they laughed.

"He's not happy," said Henry. Stella had set the bowl of water in the cage, but the bird stepped in it, spilling the water. She handed the cracked corn to Sunflower and went for more water. Sunflower spoke to the bird and dropped the food into the cage. The eaglet pecked at it, looked up and began squawking again, louder this time.

"I don't think he likes corn," said Melody.

"Eagles eat rodents. We find meat for him."

"Hold on," said Henry, and he headed back to the kitchen. Moments later he returned with a small bowl filled with chunks of beef. "This is our supper, so don't complain when there isn't enough to go around."

They all laughed.

For the next few weeks, Melody and Sunflower took turns giving water and food to their patient. They named the bird, *Charles*. Melody knew a general by that name who was extremely dignified. She thought it befitting the regal bird.

Henry and Sunflower checked the bird frequently and after a few weeks declared it was time to remove the splint. Even though Charles was tamer now than when they first found him, they didn't want to put their hands into the cage. They draped a cloth over its head again and held it there until they removed the string. The splint fell to the ground as the bird tried to flap his wings.

"We can move cage outside. See if Charles will fly away," said Sunflower.

"If he doesn't fly away," said Melody, "maybe he'll be our guard bird. The Nichols have a guard dog and the Martins have a goose that'll chase anyone who enters their yard."

They laughed and carefully moved the cage out of the shed. Henry clipped the wire around the top of the cage and announced, "Everyone, back!"

Sunflower moved Melody and her chair away from the cage. Stella stood beside them. Henry pulled the cover off and stepped back beside his wife.

"Well, Charles," said Sunflower, "spread your wings." As though acknowledging the Indian girl, the bird stood tall, looked over the side of the cage, then stepped out. Once he was on the ground, he walked around, getting his bearings. He stretched his wings, flapped them a little, clumsily at first, then lifted up and with increasing grace, rose up and over the shed. Soaring overhead, he screeched as if in thanks and disappeared from view.

"We may have lost our guard bird, girls," said Henry reaching into the cage, "but he left a thank you gift." He picked up a feather and handed it to Sunflower. "Stella tells me she has something in the kitchen for all of us."

Sunflower picked up the white tipped feather. "This is beautiful," she said, as she pushed Melody's chair toward the house.

"Mmm! I can smell cookies," said Melody.

"They smell wonderful." Sunflower's mouth watered. She loved Stella's cookies, especially the ones with bits of nuts or fruit in them. They eagerly gobbled the still warm treats along with glasses of cold milk.

"That should hold you until supper," said Stella.

"Thank you. They were delicious," the girls said, almost in unison as they left the kitchen.

Melody and Sunflower had often talked about the day the Indian girl would leave to be with her people. "I'll miss you so much, Sunflower. I wish you could stay here forever. But I understand you need to be with your own people. I do understand. Still, I'll miss you with my whole heart. You've brought so much sunshine into my life, I know well why you were named Sunflower."

With a lump in her throat, Sunflower said, "My dear friend, I never forget you. For long time I hated being here. I missed my village and the life I had. When Charles was caged, I knew how he feel. I too feel caged. I will leave soon. I am happy we are good friends. I have new respect for people now I understand them. I pray we will meet again. Here. I give the eagle's feather to you so you will not forget me."

60

"I won't forget. I could never forget...." Melody couldn't speak as tears welled in her eyes. She reached out to hug her precious friend.

Chapter 10

Escape

At last Sunflower summoned the confidence to ask Mr. Reed's permission to leave Fort Joseph and to join her people. The preacher was surprised. He didn't understand why the girl wasn't content to live with them always.

When Mrs. Reed heard about it, she was furious and hurled insults and verbal abuses at the shocked girl. Sunflower didn't say a word. She knew the time would come when she would simply leave.

In anticipation of her departure, she'd hidden her grandmother's medicine bag at the edge of the forest. *Ohum was right. I must go to my people.*

One day the preacher asked Sunflower to come to his office. He questioned her at length. "Aren't you happy here?" he asked. "You and Melody seem almost like sisters. You have adapted to our way of life and have done well in school. Is there something bothering you, Sunflower? Is there anything you want to tell me?"

Sunflower desperately wanted to say something to him but after all, Mrs. Reed was his wife and he would be expected to side with her. She hesitated and then decided to tell the preacher that she needed to be with her people. He understood. She left his office.

When Mrs. Reed saw Sunflower leave her husband's office, she screamed, "Why aren't you doing your chores, you lazy girl?" The woman was enraged and beat Sunflower with her cane while hurling mean accusations at her.

Sunflower couldn't take any more and made a dash for the door. The crazed woman screamed, "You think you can run away but I will catch up with you."

Sunflower raced toward the forest, pausing only to retrieve her medicine bag in the thick brush. She ran without stopping. Her moccasins made not a sound as she loped along the ridge. Weaving between tall pines and massive oak trees until she could go no farther, the exhausted girl crawled beneath the sweeping branches of a blue spruce, startling a rabbit who'd been nestled there.

Her heart was beating hard and she was out of breath from running steadily. Then, as the forest became increasingly dark and trees and brush more thickly concentrated, Sunflower knew she'd be safe for the night.

Reflecting on the awful outburst of Mrs. Reed, the exhausted girl shuddered. *I will continue my journey in the morning. I didn't say goodbye to*

Melody. I know she will be disappointed but I couldn't share her mother's cruelness even though Melody often questioned my bruises. Sunflower had made light of them, saying she'd bumped against something or had fallen. She tried to be more careful about covering up the purple marks. *My friend, you didn't see your mother yell and beat me and call me terrible names. She speaks with such sweetness whenever anyone is around, it would be hard to believe she is mean only to me.*

Sighing, the girl curled up, head on her arm. She was asleep instantly and didn't hear the owl hooting, coyotes yipping in the distance, or any other night noises of the forest. Instead, she slept soundly for the first time in many nights.

She did awake, however, to hear the mourning dove while it was still quite dark. Shivering from the early morning dampness, she stretched, took a deep breath, then slung the medicine bag over her shoulder and broke into a light trot.

What is it Ohum taught me about weather, thought Sunflower?

Swallows and crows
Early morn soaring high
The day will be fine
Clear and dry

"Yes, there are the swallows. It will be a good day to travel. To survive, I must remember what my grandmother taught me."

Sunflower wanted to leave in the beginning of the *Month the Frog First Croaks*, but couldn't get away and now it was already summer. She knew if she didn't move quickly she might not complete the journey before winter.

Alternately walking and trotting, she covered many miles, stopping only occasionally for a drink of water in a running stream. Keeping the sun over her right shoulder until it was directly overhead and then to her left ensured that she was traveling north. Over one ridge after another, the brave girl continued until she was very tired. *I'm afraid Mrs. Reed will send someone to get me. Just one more hill and I will stop.* But as she crossed a rocky stream she slipped and fell. Her ankle swelled and she could barely hobble. The pain was agonizing and tears ran down her cheeks. She rested for awhile but the pain continued. The closest cover was a thicket of brambles. Sunflower managed to crawl toward it. *This will be a safe place.*

Reaching into her bag for her bone knife, Sunflower found a medicine her grandmother used for pain, wrapped in a piece of hide. She took a pinch of the dried herb and placed it in her mouth. She tried to swallow but the bitterness made her gag. *This is awful.* Some of it must have gone down though because shortly the pain subsided and she felt lightheaded.

Sunflower hacked at the thorns, being careful not to cut away too much, or her secret place would be disclosed. After a while she was able to squeeze into the brambles. Her hands were scratched and bloody from the thorns but she felt safe in the cramped shelter. Curled up, she slept fitfully, her ankle throbbing.

At first light she crawled to the stream in agony and in tears. She plunged her swollen foot into the cold water, bathed her scratched hands and splashed her face, feeling refreshed.

Before she saw it, she heard the beautiful trill. Looking toward the sound, Sunflower's breath caught in her throat upon seeing the stunning bird on the outstretched branch of a tree. Its feathers were the crimson of a setting sun. It wore a cap of black as it sang. A warmth surrounded Sunflower as she sensed her grandmother's love and was comforted. *Aha! So this is what Ohum meant.* Sunflower understood at last. *I will call it the Remembrance Bird!*

Sunflower stayed in the thicket for several days, munching on pemmican and a few blackberries until she was ready to continue her journey. The swelling in her ankle had subsided but it was still tender so when she found a small but sturdy branch, she used it as a walking stick. She walked awhile and then rested, propping up her ankle so it wouldn't swell. A few days later, she felt better and was able to walk for longer periods of time but she continued using the walking stick.

Chapter 11

The Cave

Being in the forest was healing to the Indian girl's spirit and inner balance. It was peaceful and quiet, and except for an occasional rabbit or bird; a solitary time. In her village, Indians or *Original People*, as they were also known, were encouraged to spend time alone to sort out their thoughts and fears.

In the Fort Joseph village there had been little time for it. People were always around. Some days her head spun from the incessant chatter and general noise. It almost seemed like it was not a good thing to be quiet. Sunflower longed for quietude and at last she found it.

Day after day, she continued her northward journey until she was sure no one followed. "I hope they have forgotten me by now. I must stop. My moccasins are wearing thin and my dress is in tatters," mumbled the bedraggled girl. She found what she thought of as a perfect hideaway. The crest of a mountain, with a wide view below was an ideal spot with a small cave hidden behind a huge boulder.

Sitting near the entrance of the cave, Sunflower took in her surroundings. Except for the immediate area, which was rocky, the forest below was thick with pine, aspen and birch trees. She could hear the rippling of a nearby brook. The day was warm with only a few puffy clouds dotting the blue sky and she felt a sense of belonging for the first time since the village disaster.

The cave was just the right size for a single person traveling alone. Sunflower gathered moss and pine boughs to make a soft bed, cut and fashioned a noose from a vine, then honed her knife until it was sharp once more. The pemmican was nearly gone and she longed for fresh meat. She set the noose trap and baited it with a few berries. Soon she caught a rabbit. Quickly, Sunflower reset the trap. She needed meat and would use the pelt. With her sharpened knife she carefully removed the hide from the dead rabbit and stretched it over a branch to cure. By then the fire was hot enough to cook the meat. That evening she ate well.

She checked her trap again in the morning and was happy to see another rabbit. She prepared it the same as she did the first, again drying the hide.

Sunflower went to the stream for water and when she knelt to drink, she saw her image reflected. It startled the proud girl. Her hair, usually smooth and braided, was now tangled and dirty. She plunged into the stream. It felt cool and refreshing. She loosened her braids, shed her clothes and taking handfuls of sand, scrubbed her garments, then her body. She wrung the water out of her ragged clothing and hung them on a bush to dry.

Then Sunflower swam and floated until her scratched and bruised body felt renewed. Her clothes were still damp when she finished, so she carried them to the cave and spread them on the warm rocks to dry.

During the next few days Sunflower repaired her dress and lined her moccasins with the rabbit skins. Next, she made a basket by first soaking the reeds she'd gathered near the stream. When they were pliable, she split them with her fingernail and wove them into a small but watertight basket, complete with a handle. She was pleased with the results.

Although the cave was comfortable, Sunflower knew she would have to leave soon if she wanted to get to the Great Lakes People before the arrival of *The Month When Trees Crack with Cold.* The view from the cave was lovely and peaceful and she was reluctant to abandon it. "I will leave in two more days," she said.

Facing west, Sunflower saw sunsets that were reminiscent of her father's stories. They went on and on, ever changing, ever more lovely. She felt peaceful although somewhat sorrowful after an especially beautiful sunset. She still missed her family, her grandmother and her friend. "I wish Melody could see this," she said. "She would love the view and might even paint a picture of it." Sunflower reached into her medicine bag and pulled out a long cylinder. She carefully unrolled the fox painting. *My friend, how I miss you. I know you understand I had to go to my people, but I wish I could have said goodbye to you.*

Sunflower felt sad and lonely. Happy thoughts of days spent with Melody made her smile, but when ugly images of that last scene with Mrs. Reed invaded her mind, she brushed them aside, rolled up her canvas and quickly put it back into her bag. She had a hard time getting to sleep that night as her mind kept wandering and wondering. Feeling tired the following day, she dozed in the morning sun after eating a meager breakfast of berries.

A loud crash startled her. She scrambled to the back of the cave, her heart beating rapidly. *Is someone trailing me? Will they notice the basket I left? Did I leave other signs?* Cautiously, Sunflower crept to the cave entrance and listened. *It doesn't sound like man.* She shuddered. *Sounds more like a bear, a wounded one.* Sunflower stayed under cover for several minutes.

When she did venture from the darkness of the cave all was quiet. *I should bring in my basket. It might not be a bear.* She paused. This time she heard a moan. Sunflower hesitated. *Is Mrs. Reed searching for me? I can still hear her voice when she said, 'you can run away but I will catch up with you.' But what if someone is hurt?* Torn between protecting herself and helping another, her concern for others won over. She followed the noise, her heart pounding and her skin like gooseflesh.

72

A musky odor, much like that of a polecat, permeated the wooded area. The bulky form was black and lay very still. *Was that what I heard?* Nervously, the girl took a step closer. She could see the face of the bear. Even though its eyes were open it could not see. It was dead. Cautiously, she approached the beast but jumped when she heard the moan again. There, on the other side of the bear, lay a young man. He appeared to be badly mauled and unconscious. Heart still pounding, Sunflower rushed to his side and quickly assessed the wounds. His arm was ripped from shoulder to elbow. A gash sliced across his cheek and into his hairline and he was bleeding badly.

Afraid to move him, Sunflower dashed back to the cave, grabbed her medicine bag as well as the water basket and raced back. Carefully, she dabbed at the bloody arm with a piece of her tattered dress. She knew what her grandmother would do. *I have never sewn living flesh. I only watched Ohum…but I must do it*. She was nervous. Taking a deep breath, she said half-aloud, "I'll pretend I'm sewing a garment for Ohum, that way I know it will be right."

Retrieving her bone needle from the bag and snatching a hair from the injured man's head, Sunflower threaded the needle and commenced to close the gaping wound. She didn't know if this young man would live or not but surely he would bleed to death if she didn't try to help him.

It took many stitches to repair his arm and Sunflower was glad her patient was still unconscious.

Once in a while though he jumped when Sunflower's needle pierced his skin. It was then that the Indian girl remembered a soothing melody, a lullaby really. She hummed the song her Grandmother had sung to her and her brothers. The young man relaxed once more.

> *Lu-la lu-la lu-la lay*
> *Sleep my child, on this day's end*
> *May the stars protect you*
> *And the moon guide your way*
> *Lu-la lu-la lu-la lay*

Sunflower's back ached from bending over so long. She stood and stretched, then proceeded with the facial wounds, being careful to make many fine stitches so the scar would be thin. She was pleased when she finished.

Next, she gathered kindling to build a small fire. When it was blazing, she added several stones and before long they were red hot. Carefully lifting them with a sturdy branch, the girl dropped the hot stones into her water basket. Soon the water was steaming. Reaching into her medicine bag, Sunflower removed a piece of bark and put it into the hot water. She stirred the mixture until it was cooled, then poured it over the wound to help it to heal. Again, she sang the lullaby. And again the young man slept.

Sunflower stood, stretched, then went to work on the bear. Although she'd never skinned a bear, she had seen it done often enough to know how to proceed and was thankful her knife was sharp. It took a long time and she was weary beyond belief. Every muscle in her body ached but she also felt a sense of accomplishment because now she'd have food and soon a warm bearskin to sleep under. As the fire smoldered, Sunflower gathered pine boughs and covered the young man who was now snoring. She trudged back to her cave dwelling, carrying the choicest meat. Later she dragged the heavy bearskin. She was grateful to rest at last.

When dawn broke she was beside her patient once more. He moaned, opened his eyes and looked around.

"You feel better?" asked Sunflower. "What is your name? Where is your home? Are you alone in the forest?"

"Jeremy," he slurred, trying to get up.

"Jeremy. Don't try to get up. Stay until you feel better."

Jeremy closed his eyes momentarily then asked, "Who are you?"

"My name is Sunflower. But why are you in the forest? Where is your home?"

"One question at a time I answer," he said, struggling to sit up. Sunflower helped him to a sitting position. He continued, "I am Jeremy LaFontaine. I live in a small village near Toronto. I am *Chippewah* and French/Canadian. The summer I have spent alone trying to decide if I am to be Indian or Canadian, not both."

"Why?" asked Sunflower. "Why can't you be both?" She handed him the water basket and he drank.

When finished he answered, "It is difficult living with the *Chippewah*. They look down on me saying I am a half-breed. I do not like that. When I stayed with my father's brother and the Jesuits, they too called me a half-breed. I don't belong, no matter where I live." He tried to stand but his head spun and his legs were rubbery. Sunflower grabbed him as he reeled.

"I will be back," she said and went back to the cave, returning with food. After he ate, she told him to rest and covered him again with the pine boughs.

Later in the day, Sunflower checked on Jeremy. He got up and tried to walk around.

"Let me help you. In a few days you will be better, then you can leave."

The sky was becoming increasingly gray and within moments the rain came, large, heavy drops fell at first, changing to a downpour. She helped the young man to the cave. Weak from his ordeal, he managed to hobble up the hill with her assistance.

Sunflower had lugged the choicest bear meat into the cave, but the intestines needed to be cut and dried to make rope with which to stretch the hide. She dragged the heavy hide fur-side down and draped it over the rocks, hoping the rain would wash away the musky odor of the bear, but it only intensified the stench. She hung the intestines near her small fire to dry.

For the next few days Sunflower continued to bathe Jeremy's wounds with the walnut bark solution. Later in the week she removed the stitches. First she snipped the knot, then using the shell of a river clam as tweezers pulled out the hair sutures. The scars were bright pink but she knew that they would fade in time. Jeremy felt stronger and was also curious about this talkative young maiden who appeared to be self-sufficient.

As they worked together on the bear hide Jeremy asked, "Tell me who you are? Why are you here? Where is your family?"

"One question at a time," laughed Sunflower. She then related her story: "I am traveling north to meet with my tribe members who are with the Big Lakes People. Do you know them?"

"I know where the Big Lakes People live. They are not far from my mother's village. I could show you where they are."

"Thank you, Jeremy. Tell me why you are called Jeremy? It doesn't sound like an Indian name."

"You are a clever girl. Since I am only part Indian, my parents couldn't agree on a name. However, they knew an Englishman named Jeremy whom they both admired and named me after him."

Sunflower chuckled. "That is a good compromise. I will continue my journey in a day or two. You could join me. Perhaps you can help me find my people. And will you help me with the bearskin?"

"There you go again with all the questions. Yes, yes, and yes." he laughed.

The journey was easier for Sunflower now that she had a companion. Jeremy had a pleasant nature and told many stories. One was the Legend of Maple Sugar.

> *"It seems that one day Grandmother Nokomis showed Manoby how to tap trees to collect sap. It flowed in pure thick syrup. This is not good, thought Manoby. People will not have enough work if sugar is made so easily. It must be more difficult or they will fall into idleness. So he climbed to the top of the highest tree and sprinkled rain over the trees, diluting the syrup so it would flow from the trees in a thin sap.*
>
> *Thereafter, people had to work hard to make sugar. First, wood had to be cut for the fire and bark vessels were made. Next sap was collected and boiled for many nights before it became sugar."*

Sunflower laughed. "I cannot imagine anyone being lazy living in the forest. There are so many things to do, just to survive!"

Deciding it would be best to travel along the river, the pair started on their journey. For the next few weeks they made good progress but one day

Jeremy pointed to a flock of *Kaak*, wild geese, flying in a "V" formation, honking all the while on their southern flight.

"When these birds honk it means wet weather," said Jeremy, looking for a place to stop. They took refuge under the low branches of a spruce tree just as the rains came. It rained for several more days. When Sunflower and Jeremy finally emerged from their shelter, the weather had changed drastically. Icicles dripped from the trees and a skim of ice had formed on the river. It seemed that winter was upon them.

"It is too soon, Jeremy. Food will be scarce if we stay here any longer." Sunflower looked at her dress. It was ragged and she was missing a large piece of the skirt that she had torn off to tend Jeremy's wounds.

"I will be back," said Jeremy and left. When he returned, he carried a small doe over his shoulder. Together, they removed the hide. Sunflower cooked a roast over the fire while Jeremy scraped the soft tissue from the deerskin. When the meat was done, they enjoyed a hot meal and relished every bite. That night they slept with full stomachs for the first time in days.

Each morning, Jeremy stretched, pulled and rubbed the deer hide until it was soft and pliable. They worked on it together until it was ready to be made into a garment.

Taking her bone knife, Sunflower carefully cut the hide to form a dress. She sewed it together with rushes they found beside the river. Then she ducked behind a tree to change.

"Now you look more like a Lenni Lenapé," Jeremy said with a chuckle.

"And now we must make up the lost time. We cannot stop until nightfall."

Jeremy agreed. They continued their trek along the river and stopped when they came upon an abandoned canoe. Jeremy was excited. "Look at this, Sunflower. I think we can travel more easily on the water."

"I don't know how to make the canoe swim," said the girl.

"Let me fix it up, then I will show you how to paddle it. I promise it will be faster than walking."

At first, trying to maneuver the paddle was difficult for Sunflower. She felt clumsy and kept splashing herself as well as Jeremy but within hours got into a rhythm and together they moved rather swiftly. They fished for trout and bass, which were easily caught. When they stopped for the night, they cooked the fish over a fire beside the river.

Afterward Jeremy told Sunflower how his people were master canoe makers.

"How do they make the canoes?" asked Sunflower.

"They use sheets of birch bark fastened to a cedar frame, then sew them together with roots. After that they spread gum from the pine tree over the seams, making it watertight. Our people often decorate the outside of the vessels, making beautiful canoes."

"I would like to see them. This one surely isn't beautiful."

"One day you will see them."

Theirs wasn't a pretty canoe but luckily, Jeremy had to make only a few minors repairs. He knew it would be strenuous traveling upstream, but still thought it would be faster than walking.

The following day went well and Sunflower related the story of *Long Nose*, the masked cannibal who kidnapped children.

"We children were never punished. Fear that Long Nose would carry us away guaranteed our good behavior."

Jeremy laughed. "We learned of Long Nose too. I can picture him with his long scraggly beard and short skinny legs."

They covered many miles during this time, as the weather became mild again even though nights were cold. They were happy to have the bearskin and although it was still smelly, it kept them warm.

Once they came across a beaver dam that nearly blocked the narrow river but instead of destroying it, they picked up the canoe and lugged it over land until they could again launch it.

"I don't want to destroy their work. They have a right to the river," said Jeremy.

"I agree," said Sunflower. "They need to build their homes. Beavers serve a purpose in the nature of things."

The couple was developing strong muscles from paddling the canoe. With a diet of fish, an occasional rabbit or squirrel and berries that were still plentiful, they were healthy as well.

Chapter 12

The Stranger

Jeremy pulled the canoe to the edge of the river and picked up his bow. "Maybe we should stop for a while. I'll hunt for food. Perhaps I'll even get a pelt. It's cold now and I fear it will become even colder." After pulling the canoe onshore, Jeremy left, only to return a few moments later, out of breath. "I need your help. I came across an old man not far from here. He is hurt. Come with me."

Sunflower grabbed her medicine bag and followed Jeremy.

"He has a strange-looking horse. This one has long ears but it isn't a rabbit."

"What are you talking about, Jeremy?"

He laughed. "It's a mule, not a horse. I thought of your story of *Ronie* right away. The mule wore a halter and a pack was tied to its saddle so I knew someone was nearby. I circled around and found the old man on the ground. This way, through the brush."

Sunflower was puzzled. They hadn't seen another person in all this time. She knew they had gone too far for anyone from Fort Joseph to find her. "Who is he?"

"I think he's a mountain man, or maybe a trapper." They came to the man. "Hey, Mister, I brought my friend. She's a...well, kind of a doctor. Tell her what happened. Tell her what hurts."

As she walked past the mule, Sunflower petted it, saying, "Good boy."

The stranger was sitting on a rock, holding onto his leg. He wore a dirty felt hat with the brim turned down over his long hair. His beard was untrimmed but his clothing, although poorly made, looked warm enough.

"Hey, Doc. I reckon my leg is broked. Jackie here got spooked. He reared and I fell off and onto the rocks. "

Sunflower approached him. "Whew," she said half-aloud. *He smells worse than our bearskin.* She knelt in front of the man and felt his leg. "Can you stand, if I help you?" she asked.

"If'n I could stand, I wouldn't be here. "

Sunflower ignored the remark, reached into her medicine bag, removed her knife then reached for his pant leg.

"Hey, what are ya doin'?"

"I need to look at your leg. You can fix your pants later." She split the pant leg and examined him. "Yes, it looks like your leg is broken. You have a nasty cut as well. I think we can set it but I won't lie to you, it will hurt.

84

"I'm gonna need my whiskey. In the cabin. Kin you get it?" he said, looking at Jeremy.

Jeremy quickly glanced at Sunflower who mouthed, *yes*. "Where's the cabin?"

"It ain't far. Jest up the mountain a piece. You can take Jackie if you want."

"I've never ridden a mule. I'll walk. Is the whiskey inside the cabin?"

The man nodded in reply, looked at his leg and moaned once more.

While Jeremy was gone, Sunflower gathered sticks for a fire. She needed to heat water for a bark immersion to cleanse the wound as it was already starting to ooze.

"When did you fall?"

"Don't know. Coupla days, maybe more."

Sunflower cleared a spot beside the rocks for the fire, laid kindling in a teepee shape and struck her flint. It sparked, then smoldered. She blew on it, added a few more sticks and soon it was burning nicely. Next, she added stones. Then, from her bag she pulled a piece of leather and unfolded it. Inside was the bark of the white willow she used as an antiseptic.

"I will be back," she said to the man. Looking for a supply of water, she found a small rivulet coming down from the mountain and off the rocks. She tasted the liquid, then took her water basket, filled it and returned.

Bending beside the man she gave him water along with a bit of pemmican to chew. Next, with the help of a forked branch, she placed the hot stones into the water. Steam billowed from the little basket. After a few minutes she removed the stones and put them back into the fire, then added the willow bark to the water. Taking a piece of suede leather from her bag, she soaked it in the solution, wrung it out slightly and prepared to lay it over the man's wound.

The stranger tried to stop her. "Hey, Doc, will it hurt?"

"No, it won't hurt at all." She put the piece of suede over the wound, then looked up the mountain when she heard Jeremy half running, half jumping down the hill, and carrying a stone jug.

He was smiling. "I got it. Here you go," he said, handing the jug to the mountain man who quickly pulled the stopper and drank long and hard from the container. "Aaah. That's what I need." He looked at his leg. "Nope, maybe I'm needin' more."

Sunflower signaled to Jeremy and moved out of the man's hearing. "It won't be easy to set his limb. We'll need the mule to help us. Find a rope. I will tell you what to do. Even if he screams, do what I tell you. Can you do that?"

"Yes." Jeremy found a length of rope hooked over the saddle. He tied one end securely to the saddle horn and gave the other to Sunflower who looped it around the man's ankle.

"Hey, whatcha doin'? You gonna hang me?"

"No," she laughed. "We are going to set your leg and I will need your help. What's your name?"

"Jethro. Jethro Stevens."

"Mr. Stevens, take a drink from the jug, then put your arms around this rock and hold on with all your strength. I have to pull your leg to set the bone."

The man took another swig from the jug, grabbed hold of the big rock with both arms. "Ready, Doc. And call me Jethro."

Sunflower signaled for Jeremy to lead the mule slowly away while she maneuvered the broken limb into place. The man screamed in pain and let out a mouthful of curses. Still he held onto the rock. Sunflower told Jeremy to keep moving and soon the bone popped into place.

Stop," she yelled.

The man let go of the rock and slumped into a state of shock. Sunflower poured more of the antiseptic solution over the wound, covered it with the suede piece, then took two strong dried branches and placing them on either side of the leg bound them with rawhide.

"Is he dead?" asked Jeremy.

"No, but he should sleep for a while. I know it hurt when we pulled on his leg." she said wiping sweat from the man's forehead. "We cannot leave him like this. We'll have to tend him for a few days. Maybe we can take him to his cabin."

"Let me see what we can use to carry him." Jeremy left, returning shortly with large pine branches. "We can make a travois from this." He hesitated. "On second thought I don't think it will work. We can't drag him, it's too rocky. We'll have to carry him instead."

"Do you think we can get him into the saddle? His leg could hang down and it wouldn't get bumped around."

"He's not a big man, so I think between the two of us, we could hoist him up."

The man groaned and again reached for the jug of whiskey.

"Not just yet, Jethro," said Sunflower retrieving the jug. "We need to get you to your cabin first."

Jethro groaned again and let out another string of expletives.

Jeremy led the mule closer to Jethro. "I don't know how we can get him on the mule's back."

"I know," said the man, "Hey, Jackie, my boy, help Jethro. Lie down, so I can get on."

The mule nudged Jethro's arm and nickered. Then it did just what the mountain man asked. It lowered its head, then tucked its legs under its body.

"That is amazing. I've never seen an animal that can understand like this one. We will help you, Jethro." Jeremy put his arms under Jethro's and lifted him to a standing position. Meanwhile, Sunflower got on the opposite side, reached across and held Jethro's broken leg while lifting him into the saddle.

Jethro again spoke to his mule and it stood. Grabbing the reins, Jeremy led them up the mountain.

The cabin was built of logs, chinked with mud and straw. Next to it was a crude lean-to for the mule and on the broken fence beside the cabin lay a pile of pelts. They appeared to be beaver, muskrat, and raccoon. On the ground were several traps.

As they got to the cabin, the mule again lay down so Jethro could be removed and carried inside. Sunflower opened the cabin door. A bunk bed against the back wall was covered with many pelts. A wood stove occupied the center of the room. They helped Jethro into the cabin and settled him onto the bed. Sunflower propped his leg on a pile of pelts while Jeremy went to feed the mule.

Jeremy raced back down to the river and filled a bucket with water. He gave some to the mule along with grain he found in a barrel in the lean-to. The mule whinnied its thanks.

Jethro was propped up on the bed when Jeremy returned to the cabin.

"Gimme the jug," the man said. Jeremy handed it to him and the man took a swig, then held it out to Jeremy.

"No, thanks," said Jeremy as he filled the stove and started a fire.

Sunflower asked, "Jethro, how did you ever get your mule to do that trick?"

"Oh, that ain't no trick, Doc. Sometimes, when I drunk too much, I can't get on Jackie's back. After a while, he learned to squat so I could."

"That is quite a feat." She surveyed the room. "Do you have any food? We can make a meal for you."

The man pointed to a metal chest. Inside it was a supply of flour and salt but that was all. Jeremy left with his bow and arrow and soon returned with a rabbit. Taking some of the herbs from her medicine bag, Sunflower sprinkled them over the meat and cooked it on the stove. The aroma permeated the cabin. She found a couple of tin plates and two forks, went outside and rinsed them with the bucket of water Jeremy had placed there. She then filled a plate for the mountain man.

Jeremy placed a pillow behind Jethro's back and handed him the plate.

"Smells good 'nuf to eat," he said gulping down the food. "It's gettin' dark. You wanna stay here?"

"That would be nice," said the girl. "We will stay with you for a few days to be sure you are okay."

"I'll be all right but you can stay jest the same."

Jeremy trudged back down the mountain, refilled the water bucket, retrieved their gear and set it on the floor in the cabin. Again Sunflower bathed Jethro's wound once more before settling him in for the night.

She and Jeremy placed their bearskin on the floor and covered up with Jethro's pelts. It was warm in the cabin and it felt good for a change.

For the next few days, they tended to Jethro's wound. He told them wonderful stories of his life in the woods. Pretty soon he tried to hop on one foot but it was difficult to maintain his balance. Jeremy found the man's axe in the lean-to, chopped down a small maple tree and fashioned a crutch for Jethro.

90

"Hey, that will be good. Thanks."

"Your leg seems better and you can get around with the crutch so we'll leave tomorrow morning," said Sunflower.

"Okay, but you kin stay long as you want. Doc, I give you pelts to keep you warm on your trip. Hey you, Frenchie, bring me six good pelts from the rack outside."

"You don't have to, Jethro. We don't have money, so cannot pay for them."

"Hey, I give 'em to you. You fix my leg and it feels durn good."

Chapter 13

Winter Comes Too Soon

"The extra pelts will come in handy as the weather becomes colder," remarked Sunflower. The furs were heavy but by carrying them over their shoulders they were comfortable. Too soon the weather turned frigid.

Eventually they got back to their canoe where ice now clogged the water, making it difficult to maneuver. By leaning over the bow of the canoe, Sunflower poked at the ice with her paddle. The ice was especially thick in places so when it broke, Sunflower lurched forward and into the icy water.

"Aiee! It's c-c-c-cold!" she screeched. As she struggled to get her balance she kept falling back in. The water was freezing and she couldn't catch her breath.

Luckily they were still near the edge of the river and the water wasn't too deep. Very cold, but not so deep. Jeremy helped her onto the shore and quickly built a fire before handing her the bearskin.

"Give me your clothes. I will place them by the fire," he said, turning his face away from her.

Shivering so much she could barely speak, the freezing girl removed her sopping wet clothes and wrapped the fur tightly around herself.

Later, when her things were dry, she dressed. "I think we need to stop, Jeremy. We need warmer clothing," she said.

"We have enough pelts to clothe both of us," said Jeremy, holding up beaver and deerskins. He spread the pelts out and they cut and fashioned leggings as well as hooded jackets. They left the hair on the outside of the jackets so it would repel ice and snow but placed the fur on the inside of their leggings to keep them warm.

"This feels so much better," said Sunflower, pulling on the leggings. "I have finally stopped shivering." She stood. "Jeremy, just a few days ago the weather was mild and now it is cold. Do you think we will get to the Big Lakes before winter is full upon us?"

"Winter is coming on rapidly, my friend. I think we'll be in the midst of it before we get to your people. But we'll survive if we are careful."

That night they slept beneath the upturned canoe for protection against the biting wind. The river was now completely frozen over so at daybreak they decided to abandon the canoe. By continuing their pace of walking, then trotting while keeping the river in sight, they covered many miles and were warmer too. They were hampered by the heavy pelts, but felt they needed them for warmth.

One night they crawled under the branches of a large blue spruce tree. "This reminds me of the first night of my journey," Sunflower exclaimed. "I scrambled under branches just like these, hiding in case someone followed. It was comfortable. I think we will be warm here."

In the morning they awoke to a transformed world. It had snowed during the night and a blanket of white covered everything. Brushing the heavy flakes from their gear, they climbed the ridge to hike there, but the wind shrieked through the trees making it more difficult and soon it began to snow again, coming down hard at times. And now they couldn't see the river from the ridge so they slid down the embankment and found it easier to navigate next to the river The wind didn't seem as harsh there either.

By the time they stopped for the day, the snow was blowing all around them. Finding shelter under a rock ledge they pulled the bearskin over their heads. Sunflower shivered and Jeremy reached for her. They huddled together for warmth, then suddenly Jeremy kissed her on the mouth.

She jerked away. "Please Jeremy, do not kiss me. I like you. I think we're good friends but I am not ready for this." Jeremy said not a word but turned away, his back now to her. Eventually they slept.

When the storm subsided they gathered their belongings and trudged silently through the snow that was becoming deep. They tired easily. Finding another outcropping of rock they placed their gear down to rest. Jeremy left without a word.

He must need to be by himself, thought Sunflower. I know he is upset. I did like his kiss but I want him only as my friend.

Searching through the snow for kindling, she built a small fire, honed her bone knife until it was sharp once more then picked up a piece of hide that Jeremy had softened. She cut a long strip of the leather and taking a piece of rawhide, she split it and sewed the piece into a long pocket.

Next, she retrieved her treasured painting that was becoming battered in the bag. Sliding it into the leather pocket, it fit perfectly. *This will protect it.* She slipped it back into her medicine bag.

Returning, Jeremy stood beside Sunflower, his head hung low. He spoke softly. "I am sorry, Sunflower. I shouldn't have kissed you. I want us to continue to be friends. It will be too difficult to travel if we aren't. I promise I won't do it again."

"I understand," said Sunflower. "I too want us to be friends."

Jeremy looked around. "I'm glad you made a fire. We will need it for this task." He set his bundle of wood down, added a few dried pieces to the fire, then cut his green wood into strips. Wetting the bundle with melted snow, he steamed the pieces over the fire until they were pliable before bending them into loops. Next, taking strips of bear gut to form a webbing, Jeremy made two pairs of snowshoes.

96

"This is wonderful," said Sunflower admiring the strange contraptions, "but I have never worn them. We didn't travel much in the winter."

Jeremy put the shoes on Sunflower's feet and helped her up. She tried to walk but every few steps, tripped and fell. She got up and tried again. Frustrated because she kept falling she cried, "How do you do it, Jeremy? What is the secret?"

Jeremy laughed at the sight of Sunflower trying to walk in the snowshoes. At first, Sunflower was upset that he laughed at her. She felt frustrated at herself for being clumsy, but then she saw the humor in it and laughed too. It broke the tension between them.

Helping Sunflower to her feet again, he showed her how to walk. "There is no secret. Just take one step at a time, but be careful not to step on the back of the shoe. It will take practice before you can do it easily but you won't sink into the deep snow."

In time she got used to the long shoes. *Jeremy is right, it is faster walking on top of the snow.*

Weeks passed and Sunflower developed a cough. She became weak and often perspired even though she shivered with cold.

"Do you want to stop for a while?" ask concerned Jeremy.

"I don't know. If I sleep, maybe I'll feel better." Her head ached as did every bone and muscle in her body. It was difficult to put even one foot in front of the other.

Jeremy made a fire, spread the buckskin on the ground and pulled the pelts over Sunflower. She soon fell asleep. Jeremy searched the woods for something to ease her cough, but he didn't know what to look for.

A wave of nausea woke the girl and she plodded through the deep snow to a nearby thicket where she was sick to her stomach. Staggering back to the fire, she crawled back under the bearskin but had barely put her head down when stomach pains gripped her and she ran back to the thicket. Three times she was sick. The last time, when she stood to go back, she reeled in dizziness. *Why is the ground spinning? What is happening?* Then she fell unconscious.

When Jeremy returned he didn't see his traveling partner. Her snowshoes were beside the campfire as was her medicine bag. "Sunflower, where are you?" he called. There was no answer. He followed her footprints. He didn't find her but saw where she'd been sick. Worried, he called once more. He noted her footprints weren't in the direction of the fire. *Is she looking for me?* Again he called out her name but there was no response.

He carefully retraced each step she had taken before he noticed a drop off the side of the mountain. With panic in his voice he cried, "No." Picking up a long dead branch he dropped it over the side and raced to the bottom of the embankment.

When he caught sight of the stick that marked the place, he trudged through the snow. He began to dig, slowly at first, then frantically. His arms became tired and his hands were freezing but he kept on. Just as he was about to abandon the task, he found a moccasin and gasped, "Sunflower!"

Digging carefully and brushing away the snow he found her at last. He thought she was dead. Her skin had a bluish tinge and she was still. He moved closer and put his head to her chest. He detected a faint heartbeat. Carrying her through the snow to a flat area, Jeremy placed her down gently, removed his own jacket and covered her. He then raced back up the hill, stomped out the small fire he'd made earlier, and retrieved their gear.

He spread a fur on the ground as a bed for the frozen girl and layered other furs on top of her. He commenced to build another fire, stopping periodically to check on Sunflower. Although she was breathing, she was still unconscious. Jeremy said half aloud, "I want to make a tea but I don't know which remedy to use. Maybe plain warm water will help." Leaning over her, he rubbed her hands trying to get warmth into them. Much later, Sunflower opened her eyes.

"I was worried. Here, drink this." He propped her head. She was weak but sipped the water. When she tried to speak, Jeremy stopped her. "Don't talk, my little friend. Just take it easy."

He made the decision to stay there for the night, thinking she might feel better by morning. He cut pine boughs and made a shelter. At first light, he checked on her. She was still sleeping. He stoked the fire, then left to find something for her. When he returned she was still sleeping but every so often had a coughing spell. When at last she awoke, Jeremy was roasting a small rodent. He gave some meat to her but she only picked at it.

They camped in the gully for three more days. Sunflower was still ill. Her cough was so deep it appeared to come from her toes. She seemed depressed as well. Jeremy tended to her as best he could, giving her sips of water and encouraging her to eat.

One morning he returned with breakfast, excited. "Sunflower," he called.

"What is it?" She was dizzy as she tried to sit up.

"Look. Feel it. It is so soft and warm."

"Oh, no! Not, a fox fur," she wailed and bent over, her head in her arms.

Jeremy knelt beside her. He couldn't understand why she was so upset. "Did I do something wrong, *mon ami*?"

"No, Jeremy. How could you know?" Sunflower cried, struggling to hold her head up. "I told you about Melody, but I didn't show you the painting she made for me. In my medicine bag you'll find a leather pocket." He reached for the bag and removed the item.

"Open it, please."

100

Pulling the cylinder out of the pocket, he untied the ribbon and unfurled the painting. "Why, it's the fox. This is the painting she made for you? She's a good artist and now you will have the soft fur, to remind you of her."

"Oh." Sunflower paused, her hand to her head. "I didn't think of it that way. Perhaps you are right." She closed her eyes and put her head down again. *I don't feel well. My head pounds. Great Manito, this is hard for me. The fox fur reminds me of all I have been through. I don't want to go on. Take my spirit so I can be with Ohum and my brothers and my father.* Then she slept. When she awoke later, still feeling dreadful, she said to Jeremy, "Leave me here. I cannot go on. I am too sick."

At first shocked, then upset, Jeremy said, "You can't give up now. We've been through the worst of it and should be at my village in a few more days. You are always ready to heal others; don't you have something in your medicine bag for a cough? Can't you find something to make yourself well? I don't understand. Why do you want to give up?"

Sunflower had been sick and delirious, too weak to even think, until Jeremy reminded her. She hadn't even thought about healing herself. Lifting her head she said, "You are right. I do have a cough remedy."

Jeremy handed her the bag. She poked through it, searching until she came up with the white oak bark Ohum had often used for cough and fevers. "We need to make a tea," she said, weakly.

"I can do that." Jeremy stoked the fire, then filled the water-tight basket with snow. He went to the river and dug out a couple of small stones that he placed in the fire. When they were hot, he dropped them into the basket. The snow melted but the water was not warm. He repeated the process by reheating the stones, until the water was hot. Jeremy took the bark and immersed it, letting it steep. Handing it to her he said, "It's hot."

Sunflower blew on the steaming liquid, inhaled its aroma and sipped the tea. She inhaled again. She stopped. She lifted her head and listened as she heard the trill in the tall pine. There, against a backdrop of white, was the brilliant *Remembrance Bird.* Sunflower knew then it was a sign from her grandmother that she would get well. "Thank you, Ohum." she whispered.

"What did you say, Sunflower?"

"Oh, nothing. I don't know why I didn't think of this medicine before. I guess I was feeling sorry for myself."

They rested for the remainder of the day. Sunflower continued to sip the tea and sleep. By morning, she felt better even though she was too weak to walk. Jeremy fashioned a travois, like the one he tried to make for the mountain man.

Sunflower resisted. "I can walk," but she collapsed shortly and relented when Jeremy insisted she ride.

"I can pull it easily in the snow," he said.

Sunflower remembered how easy it was to pull Melody on her sled. She stretched out on the pine branches after Jeremy piled on their pelts and other gear. As Jeremy towed the sled, she soon fell asleep and dreamed of being rocked in her grandmother's arms. They continued their journey stopping frequently until Sunflower was stronger. When she was able to walk for a good part of the day, they abandoned the travois.

Chapter 14

Big Water

When Jeremy spotted the body of water he pointed excitedly to Sunflower. "This is the Ontario Lake," he said excitedly.

"Are you certain? Could it be the great salt water?" She had never seen the ocean but was told it was very big.

Jeremy laughed. "No, it is not the great salt water although this is a very large lake. I know this place; I grew up not far from here. We are almost home, *mon ami*. Do you want to meet my family first or would you like to go directly to your people?"

"While traveling I was excited about seeing members of my tribe, but now I think I would like to meet your family first."

"We should be there soon," said Jeremy.

Crossing the river was no simple task, even for a spirited young man like Jeremy. If they crossed the southern end of the lake they would have to deal with the great falls so by continuing their journey north, they came to the more narrow end of the lake where there was a ferry.

"How much?" asked Jeremy.

"How much you got?" was the answer.

"I'll give you a nice pelt."

"Make it two and I'll take both of you across."

Sunflower was nervous but the ferry master took them across without incident and they continued toward Jeremy's home.

"I'd like to wash my dress and leggings before we greet your family, Jeremy."

"No, Sunflower. You can't do that. You've been ill. I don't want you to take a chance on getting sick again. The weather is foul and you still are not well. It's been a long trip. Just wait. My mother will be so happy to see us that she won't notice how untidy we are." Jeremy smiled, thinking about seeing his people again. Spending the summer in the forest by himself and now traveling with Sunflower, the young man felt more confident. He knew he wanted to live in the Indian village and his thoughts kept returning to SnapDragon, a girl just about Sunflower's age. He had decided that it really didn't matter that he was half French or half Indian, but what did matter was how he felt about himself.

"Sunflower, my friend, look…there is my mother's village!"

She faced in the direction he pointed. In the distance she could see smoke rising from the cooking fires and a faint outline of wigwams. The scene was familiar and Sunflower couldn't hold back her tears.

Jeremy's mother recognized her beloved son who walked with a companion. She waved and Jeremy raced to embrace her. Other tribe members rushed to greet Jeremy with hugs and handshakes. It was a warm and happy reunion.

Sunflower's head was spinning by the time she was introduced to all of Jeremy's relatives and friends. His mother, Smiling Face, noticed how pale her son's companion looked. Taking the girl by the hand, she led her to the wigwam, gave her a cup of herbal tea and showed her to a bed of fragrant pine boughs. Sunflower was asleep almost as soon as she finished her tea. Smiling Face covered her with a hand-woven blanket of wool.

Jeremy was anxious to share his experiences with his people. "I am too excited to rest," he said.

Tribe members remarked about the change in him. "Not only has Jeremy grown taller, but he has a sense of pride that didn't exist prior to his journey," one remarked.

Jeremy told them of the struggle with the bear and how Sunflower saved his life. They could scarcely believe he had been wounded so badly and were astonished at the smoothness of his scars. They were anxious to talk with the young woman who seemed to possess a vast knowledge of medicine.

Although Sunflower slept for the remainder of the day and night, she was extremely weak and her body ached. The journey had been especially hard on her. Jeremy was used to eating wild game and berries, having spent the summer in the forest. Sunflower's diet at Fort Joseph consisted of chicken, beef, bread, potatoes and other vegetables and her system was not accustomed to the meager diet on their journey. Painfully thin, she still had her cough.

"Stay with us until you are strong again," said Smiling Face. "Stay for the remainder of the winter before making the trip to your people."

Sunflower agreed. At first she slept for long periods of time, wakening only when Smiling Face or SnapDragon brought food to her. As the weather improved, so did Sunflower and soon she took short walks outside. When she felt better, she told the children the stories she'd learned as a child. Whenever she was outdoors, children gathered around her. One little girl gave Sunflower a bracelet she'd made from porcupine quills and pumpkin seeds.

"It is a good health charm," said the girl. "I made it myself."

"I will keep it close to me at all times," replied Sunflower, suppressing a cough and clutching the charm to her heart. As she recovered to good health, Sunflower added the weight she'd lost. Her short jaunts to help gather firewood in the brisk fresh air brought color back to her cheeks and her cough subsided somewhat.

Usually Sunflower put her good health charm next to her moccasins before going to sleep, but one morning she couldn't find it. Another morning, as she slipped her foot into her moccasin, she quickly pulled it off. It was filled with wet mud. She was puzzled but didn't tell anyone about these things. Instead, she kept a careful watch to see who might be responsible. Most of the mischief occurred while she slept so one night Sunflower piled an extra blanket under her sleeping blanket to look like someone was there. Huddled in the dark against the wall of the wigwam, she dozed for a while but was awakened by the rustle of someone entering the tent. Holding her breath and watching, she saw a small person creep over to her sleeping blanket. Sunflower jumped up and tackled the intruder.

"Yaaaaa! What are you doing?" She pulled the intruder outside and into the moonlight and was surprised it was a young girl. "Who are you?"

"Me Little Squirrel. Let me go."

"I will let go when you tell me what you are doing here."

"I hate you. You go away."

"Why do you hate me? You don't even know me. What have I done to you?"

"My people like you and are nice to you. They were good to me before you came." Again, the girl tried to escape.

Sunflower maintained her grip. "Your people are good people. They are helping me because I was sick."

"My friends gave you a good health bracelet. They don't give me one."

"Little Squirrel, why are you so angry?"

"You have many friends. You happy person. You know no sadness. My Mama died last summer and my father left after that. I have nobody."

Sunflower released the child and spoke softly. "Who do you live with?"

"I live with Basket Woman, but she has many children and doesn't see me."

"Basket Woman? I don't know her. Little Squirrel, I'm a happy person because I choose to be happy. But I do know sadness. My mother died too when I was young. Later, our village was destroyed and my little brothers were killed. Everyone died that day, except my grandmother and me."

"Why didn't you die?" Little Squirrel was showing some interest in the story.

"I was not in the village at the time so I was spared. Then soldiers took us to live with the white people. I'll tell you about that part of my life, but not now. Right now I want you to return my bracelet and tell me you won't do it again. If not, I'll tell Smiling Face. I'm sure you don't want her to know how you treated me."

The child hung her head. "Me ugly person. Won't do it again."

Sunflower reached down and hugged the little girl. "You are not an ugly person. You are angry and sad but behaving this way will not make people like you." She knelt in front of her and looked her in the eye. "Let me be your friend, Little Squirrel. I will show you how to be a happy person."

110

"I give you the bracelet now." The girl reached into her dress and handed it to Sunflower.

Sunflower smiled. "Now shoo! Go back to your sleeping blanket. We'll talk in the morning."

Little Squirrel ran back to Basket Woman's camp.

Sunflower had another coughing spell and tried to get back to sleep but kept thinking of the sad little girl who was so jealous of her. *I must help her.*

The following day Smiling Face was folding a woven blanket. "That is a beautiful blanket," said Sunflower. "Did you make it? What did you make it from?"

"See the sheep grazing in the field?" asked Smiling Face.

"I don't know that name, *sheep.* Do you mean those fuzzy animals that make a strange noise when I approach them?"

"Yes. We didn't know about sheep either until SnapDragon and her family joined our village. When they lived in the west with the Sioux tribe, they had many sheep. They brought a small flock with them. The hair on the animal's body grows long during the winter. In spring we shear it and spin it into a long thread. Sometimes we even dye it different colors, using sumac, wild onions, or the indigo plant before weaving it into a blanket or shawl."

"Jeremy showed me the weaving loom where SnapDragon was working on it. One thread went one way and another the other way. Before long, she had a piece of cloth with a beautiful design. Could you teach me to weave?"

"Yes, I will show you but you need to rest a while longer. You are still not well."

"I know. I am feeling better but must replace the remedy for my cough. I will look for it today. I used up the supply I had."

"May I come along with you?" asked Smiling Face.

"It would be an honor to have you come with me," said Sunflower.

That afternoon, not only did Sunflower have Smiling Face as a companion, but several other women as well as Little Squirrel, who were just as curious, tagged along. They gathered many useful herbs and barks. Sunflower explained about each of them.

"We never take all the herbs or roots or flowers. We need to be sure to leave enough so the plant can renew itself. This is important so we will always have a supply."

Later, Sunflower was able to show her skills at closing a wound when a young brave accidentally cut his leg while sharpening his hunting knife. This time the cut was smooth, not jagged and torn like Jeremy's. She closed it with perfect stitches, again using hair from the patient's head.

"But why do you use his hair," asked Smiling Face, "when your own is much longer?"

"If I use the hair of the injured person, he is less likely to get poisoning and the wound will heal more quickly," answered Sunflower." My grandmother taught me that but I don't remember why."

"I will try it next time because often the stitches we make become red and swollen in a few days and take a long time to heal. Thank you, Sunflower."

"I thank you, Smiling Face, for letting me stay here. I do feel stronger now and am ready to find my people."

Over the next few days, Sunflower went through the things in her bag, one by one, replacing herbs and barks as needed.

Smiling Face watched her. "What is in the leather pocket?"

"It is a painting given to me by my friend, Melody. I told you about her." Sunflower removed the cylinder, untied the red ribbon, then unrolled the painting and held it up for Jeremy's mother.

"*Wallow.* He is beautiful and looks so real."

"I know," said Sunflower. "And now my bag is organized once more and I am ready to meet with my people.

Chapter 15

My People

The day arrived for Jeremy and Sunflower to start their trek to the Big Lakes Village. The air was fresh; fields were beginning to green; new leaves had sprouted from maple trees and snow flowers created a carpet of white. Sunflower was dressed in her new skirt and tunic, gifts from Smiling Face and SnapDragon who both made and decorated the garment with quills and beads. The tawny shade of brown complemented Sunflower's bronze skin and black hair.

Feeling energetic now, Sunflower was anxious to complete her journey. She'd been comfortable in Jeremy's village but it was time to seek out her own people.

Little Squirrel approached Sunflower. "Why you leave?"

"I must go to my people."

Tears filled the child's eyes as she said, "But you won't come back."

"I will. Perhaps I will have a surprise for you when I return."

"I made a safe journey charm for you," said Little Squirrel, handing her a bracelet made from clay beads.

"Why this is beautiful. Thank you, my little friend." She hugged the girl.

Some of Jeremy's people, including Little Squirrel, accompanied them for part of the journey. As they neared the Big Lakes Village, Jeremy noticed that his companion walked more slowly and was unusually quiet. "What is wrong? You are going to see your people."

Apprehensive, she answered. "I am nervous. I don't know if anyone from my village is there. Will I know them? Will they know me? Will they welcome me? What will I say to them?"

"Don't you know they'll be excited about getting news of other tribe members? Listen, *mon ami*, you were the one who gave me strength and courage to believe in myself. Now, I'm giving you your own advice. If you are true to yourself and are the best that you can be, no one can ask for more." He hesitated. "Does that sound familiar? Didn't you say that to me? Be proud that you escaped Mrs. Reed. Be happy that you can read and write and had Melody, as a friend. You can relate the tragic news of your village to the tribe members. Even if they aren't of your village, perhaps they know of someone who is. They await news too. So stop fretting. We will be there soon."

116

At that moment a flash of red flew past Sunflower, reminding her once again of her grandmother. The presence of the red bird reassured the young girl her journey was the one she should make.

By the time the two travelers could see the village, the Big Lakes People already knew of their arrival and sent a party of braves to greet them. Sunflower was glad she'd spent the winter with Jeremy's family. She now felt strong and healthy. She'd learned and spoken English at Fort Joseph and felt she needed practice with her own language. Although Chippewah and the Lenni Lenapè languages were not exactly alike, if you knew one language you could easily converse in the other.

"Greetings my friends," said the leader. "Welcome to the Village of the Tunikani. I am Flying Eagle, son of Chief Bald Eagle."

Sunflower's heart thumped. Flying Eagle was a handsome young man, most likely the same age as Jeremy. He stood tall and straight, his jet black hair tied in back. His shoulders were muscular and he wore a fringed tunic and leggings. *Something about him reminds me of Charles, the eaglet we found.* She chuckled to herself.

Jeremy raised his right hand in the customary greeting. "I am Jeremy, or Paxinosa, as I am known in the Chippewah village. This is Sunflower, of the Lenni Lenapé Tribe."

After the greeting, Jeremy and Sunflower were taken and introduced to Chief Bald Eagle. *I know where Flying Eagle gets his good looks*, thought Sunflower. The handsome chief also had a regal air about him and wore a headdress of eagle feathers, trimmed with colorful beads over his graying hair. He was dressed in a long deerskin robe with fringe along the sleeves and hem and sat on a beaver fur cushion. He remained seated.

The tepee was large, decorated inside as well as outside with pictographs in bright colors. Sunflower felt comfortably warm and noticed they were using corncobs that burned hot but with little smoke. She made a mental note to try it some time.

Chief Bald Eagle asked Sunflower many questions. She, in turn, asked if there were any members of her tribe there.

"There were a number of them," answered the Chief, "but we had the pox sickness and it wiped out nearly our whole village. One man came alone. He was looking for his family. When he didn't find them he lost his spirit and awaits to die. We have tried to cheer him but he keeps saying, 'If only I had returned sooner I might have saved them.' The Chief stood. "Enough. We will meet again when you have eaten and rested."

Sunflower's heart pounded. She was anxious to see the people who may have been from her village, especially the one looking for his family, but it was getting late and Chief Bald Eagle dismissed them.

Jeremy and Sunflower separated. He left with a group of braves and she followed two women, Corn Blade and Quiet One. They led her to another tepee where she found warm water in which to wash as well as a lovely bearskin robe to rest upon. Sunflower was so excited she didn't think she could sleep, but after a cup of tea made from sweet grass she was soon relaxed and dozed.

A short time later she awoke feeling that someone was watching her. When she opened her eyes she saw Quiet One sitting in a corner, staring at her. Sunflower spoke but the girl turned her head, then shyly took Sunflower's hand and led her outside where a bowl of steaming hot stew and flatbread waited. The newcomer relished the delicious food.

Soon Corn Blade came for Sunflower and they returned to Bald Eagle's tepee. Jeremy was waiting for her. There were a number of people there but Sunflower didn't recognize any of them. Still, she told her story. No one came forward to tell her they were from the village and knew her or at the very least, her father or grandmother. Sunflower felt alone and afraid.

Jeremy moved next to her. "What is wrong, Sunflower?" he asked.

"I do not recognize anyone," she said solemnly. "They don't seem to know me either. Perhaps it was a mistake to come."

"You know you had to come. These people have heard of your medicine skills. They are anxious for you to see their sick people. You will feel better when you've been here a while and get to know the people."

"I think you may be right, but right now I want to take your mother's offer to return to your village. I am disappointed and sad. I want to leave soon."

Chapter 16

Answered Prayer

Bald Eagle motioned for Sunflower to approach. She did and sat when he signaled her to. Then he spoke. "Word has it that you have medicine magic, young woman. Are you willing to show us some of it?"

"With due honor, Chief Bald Eagle, I know a little of barks and herbal remedies. I have set broken limbs and sewn gaping wounds, but I do not call it magic," answered Sunflower.

"Show us your skills and we will decide if it is magic or not," said the Chief. He dismissed her with a wave of his hand.

Corn Blade led Sunflower to another tepee where numerous people on sleeping robes, were lined up one after another. As she approached the first patient, a young boy, she knelt and put her cool hand on his forehead.

"This child has a fever," she said. Jeremy anticipated her need and handed Sunflower the medicine bag. She removed a packet of maple bark and asked for a basket with warm water in which to soak the bark. She smiled lovingly at the child as she bathed his face with the refreshing solution, using a piece of doeskin as a cloth.

From one patient to the next, she asked them questions, and to some she gave the herbal drink. A commotion outside startled them and in rushed a frantic woman, with a screaming toddler in her arms. "Help me, please help my baby," she begged. They all went outside so as not to disturb the other patients. Sunflower looked at the child, and saw that the tip of her tiny finger was nearly severed.

"What happened?" she asked.

"The children have a rabbit and were feeding it. The baby poked her finger into the cage. I guess the rabbit thought it was a crispy carrot."

"Jeremy, can you help me, please?" He was immediately beside her with the medicine bag. "I will need a tea infusion of chamomile." She turned to a woman near her. "Fetch a handful of wampee leaves and rinse them well in clear water."

And to the mother, "Can you pull a long hair from your daughter's head? Do it gently, so that she isn't in needless pain." Then she took the baby in her arms and sang her lullaby song. *"Lu-la lu-la, lu-la lay, Sleep my child..."*

Jeremy returned with the warm chamomile tea and heard Sunflower singing. He handed the cup to her. She spoon fed some to the child.

"That song is familiar, but I know I didn't learn it from my mother. What is it?"

Sunflower smiled, still rocking the child. "I sang that to you when I was sewing your open wounds, Jeremy. I was so scared because I had never done it before. It was the only thing that came to mind, a lullaby Ohum sang to me when I was upset. It worked too, because you settled down and were asleep by the time I finished." She paused. "Just as this child is sleeping now."

The women returned with the wampee leaves and the child's mother gave Sunflower a long strand of hair which she threaded onto her bone needle and began to stitch the tiny finger, all the while continuing to sing.

The child slept through the entire ordeal. It was only when the finger had been bathed in a white willow solution and wrapped in the leaves and securely fastened, did she awaken. She whimpered and Sunflower handed the child back to her mother.

Corn Blade suggested that Sunflower stop and rest. "You can tend to the others tomorrow. It is nearly time for the evening meal."

Chief Bald Eagle again summoned Sunflower. Corn Blade took her by the arm and led her to him. "My people have told me how you comforted some of the sick and dying today as well as sewing the finger of a little child, who happens to be my granddaughter. I want to thank you."

"I did not know she was your granddaughter but was happy to be of help, Chief Bald Eagle. She is a brave and beautiful child."

"I am well pleased. I saw her. She was playing as if nothing had happened. Tonight we will have a feast and there will be much dancing. You and your friend will attend."

"We will be there."

Corn Blade took Sunflower back to the tepee and told her she should rest before the feast.

That evening they feasted on venison stew along with roasted corn and a strange but delicious drink. Sunflower felt a little dizzy after sipping it. "I don't know what this is, but I don't think I should drink any more of it," she told Jeremy.

Soon the dancing started. When the drums began to beat, the men, including Jeremy, formed a circle. Slowly, slowly, the rhythm increased and the women formed a circle around the men. Corn Blade took Sunflower's hand. "Come," she said. "I will show you how."

Hesitantly, Sunflower followed the girl. "Heel, toe, toe, turn, turn. Heel, toe, toe, turn, turn. That's all there is to it." Sunflower tried it and soon was caught up in the dance. Jeremy looked over at her and grinned. He seemed to be having a wonderful time as well.

It was then that she noticed Flying Eagle. He had been watching her and when she looked up he smiled. Sunflower's heart thumped even louder than before as he approached. Without a word, he took her hand. They danced and danced. Then he led her to

124

the edge of the festivities where they talked for hours, oblivious of anyone else.

"How old are you?" he asked.

"I am nearly sixteen years old." she answered.

"Years? In our village we count age in summers."

Sunflower laughed. "I lived too long with the white people I think. It is about the same as sixteen summers. And you, how old are you?"

"I am eighteen summers."

He asked her many questions. Next he said, "Do you know the child whose finger was bitten by the rabbit?"

"Your father told me it was his granddaughter." She hesitated. "Is it your child?" Sunflower was fearful of the answer.

Flying Eagle laughed. "No, that is my sister's baby."

"She is a precious being. Her finger should heal quickly." Sunflower was relieved to know it wasn't Flying Eagle's child.

Too soon the festivities ended. Flying Eagle walked her to her tepee, and said goodnight. Sunflower had pleasant dreams and awoke in the morning with a smile on her face. She followed Quiet One to the stream where they bathed before the morning meal. She was anxious to tend to the rest of the sick and ailing so that she and Jeremy could return home although now that she had met Flying Eagle, she had mixed feelings.

"Can you take me to visit the sick, Quiet One?" The girl took her to Corn Blade instead. "I want to visit the sick," she said. Corn Blade led the way. They met Jeremy on the path. He joined them as they entered the tepee to minister to the sick. The last patient was a man who was painfully thin and appeared to be in a dazed state. Sunflower put her hand on his chest, and the man looked up. He became agitated, trying to speak but Sunflower couldn't make out the words. Then she listened carefully. "Little Mouse, Little Mouse," he mumbled.

Sunflower's faced drained. She looked at Jeremy, mouth agape.

"What's wrong?" He rushed to her side.

"Little Mouse was my mother's name," whispered Sunflower. "For a moment I thought...oh never mind, it couldn't be."

Sunflower's hands trembled as she made a solution of herbs for the patient. She propped the man's head to give him the tea. He opened his eyes. Again he murmured, "Little Mouse. Little Mouse, you returned."

Sunflower chose to confront him. "I am not Little Mouse. I am Sunflower. What is your name?"

Struggling to sit up, the man became excited and exclaimed, "I am Black Robe of the *Lenni Lenapé*..."

"Father?" Sunflower was tentative. As she looked deeply into his eyes, she recognized the man. "My dear father. You are alive." Tears of joy ran

126

down Sunflower's cheeks as she wrapped her arms around the man.

"Flower that Blooms in the Sun?" The man's eyes widened. "My own dear daughter? I searched for you for many moons but finally I gave up."

"Father dear, I didn't recognize you. All this time I thought you were dead." Sunflower sat back and raised her arms "My prayers have been answered after all. Great Manito, thank you!"

"But, my daughter, tell me where you have been? What happened to you? Where are your brothers? Your grandmother?" He lay back on the cot, exhausted.

Sunflower smiled at all the questions. "My Father, the excitement may be too much for you. I will tell you everything, but first you must get well. Sleep for now." The man closed his eyes and Sunflower gazed toward the setting sun, "Then I will tell you a story."

Sunflower was overcome with joy of finding her father after all that time. That evening she and Jeremy talked for a long time. They decided that he should return to his village while she stayed to care for her father. "I will return for you after the next full moon," he said. "Perhaps your father will come back with you to my village."

"I would like that, Jeremy. Goodbye for now, my dear friend."

Sunflower continued to tend to the sick of the village. The child whose finger she had sewn was doing nicely. Most of the others had responded to the medications, but Sunflower was concerned that her father was not improving. She helped him walk outside, hoping the fresh air would help but he was too weak to stand. She gathered his sleeping robe for him lie upon, then told him what happened in their village and how she kept hoping he would find them. She related the story about the soldiers and how they rescued them but when she told him about the twins his face, already pale, turned ashen.

After a moment he drew a breath, then spoke. "When I returned to the village, I saw only charred ruins. I didn't find anyone alive. I did see what appeared to be graves. I searched the forest for weeks looking for you…for someone…anyone, and finally gave up. I had hoped that you joined with the Big Lakes People and was disappointed when you weren't here.

Sunflower told him about Melody and her family, how she attended school. She left out the parts about the mean Mrs. Reed. "As Ohum lay dying, she insisted that I go to the Big Lakes People. It was a very long trip and I could not have made it without Jeremy. I was disappointed when I didn't recognize anyone here and they didn't know of you or my family. I am happy to have found you at last."

Over the next few weeks Sunflower visited with her father during the day and told him more stories about her adventurous travels. She even mentioned Flying Eagle. Her father merely smiled.

She could see and even smell death surrounding the man. *I know his spirit will leave him*

128

soon. I must make him comfortable during his last days. I am grateful to have found him, although it is hard to see my father in this shell of a once strong man. Sunflower turned her face from her father when her tears became unstoppable.

Chapter 17

A New Language

Her father fell asleep and Sunflower sought out Quiet One. "Why do you not speak?" she asked. Quiet One lowered her head and twisted away. *Does she not hear?* Sunflower clapped her hands softly but the girl didn't turn. She clapped them together sharply. Still the girl didn't respond so she touched her arm, then Quiet One turned to look at her.

Corn Blade came by in the afternoon. Sunflower asked, "Why does Quiet One not speak?"

"She never has," said the girl.

"Doesn't she hear?"

"No, she is deaf." Corn Blade looked at her. "At first we thought she was slow…dim witted…but we learned she is bright in many ways."

Sunflower told her about SnapDragon and how she thought she might help Corn Blade.

"I will speak to the chief about her for you."

Later, Chief Bald Eagle again summoned Sunflower. "Corn Blade informs me that you can help Quiet One who doesn't hear."

"Yes, Honored One." Sunflower explained how she tried to get the girl's attention by clapping. "It wasn't until I touched her arm that she looked up. There is a woman in Jeremy's village who can speak with the deaf."

"How can she do that if the person can't hear?"

"It is a sign language, using hand gestures. Would you mind if I take Quiet One with me to the Chippewah village? Jeremy will come for me after the next full moon." She felt brave, asking the chief but felt strongly that the girl was missing out on much of life.

"Many years ago, we *Original People* had a language, before we learned to speak with our tongues, but no one uses it any more. Perhaps it would help Quiet One. When Jeremy comes, we will allow Quiet One to go with you."

Sunflower recalled how the doctor made hand gestures to communicate with her and her grandmother. *That seems so long ago, nearly a lifetime away.*

That evening, Flying Eagle visited Sunflower. "I would like to speak with you."

Sunflower's heart leaped once again. "Yes?"

"When you first arrived at our village I noticed you and the moment our eyes met I felt we were with one heart. I don't know what it is, but I think about you all the time and want to be with you." He fidgeted. "Do you mind that I am so bold?"

Sunflower laughed nervously. "No, I don't mind that you are bold. I am flattered and have to admit that my heart skips whenever I see you. Even your name gave me a thrill so now I must tell you about Charles." She related the story of the eaglet they found and how they nursed it back to health.

"I like that story. I even like the name. You can call me Charles, if you wish." He took her hand and spoke seriously. "I would like to ask your father for your hand in marriage."

"I know my father would approve. He told me that he respects your father and most of the people in the village. But I do not think I am ready for marriage, Charles. There is something I need to do first. I am just not sure what it is."

"You give me hope. I'll settle with that for now, but don't take too long deciding. I can be patient for just so long."

Jeremy arrived as promised, after the full moon. He came with news from his village. They spoke about many things. Sunflower wanted to tell him about Flying Eagle but decided to wait. Instead, she told him about Quiet One.

"SnapDragon will be delighted to see you again and I am sure she will be happy to teach the sign language to Quiet One. Speaking of her, we have been seeing a lot of each other and I think we will wed soon."

Sunflower felt her heart would burst. She'd been afraid to tell Jeremy she cared for him as a friend or brother and that Flying Eagle was the one who caught her heart. She was glad SnapDragon, of whom she also was fond, was the one he chose. "I am happy for you. When I was at your village, I could tell she liked you. Her face lit up whenever she saw you or anyone spoke of you."

Jeremy was pleased. As they prepared to leave, however, Sunflower's father worsened. She'd searched for other medicines for him, but nothing seemed to work.

"Father, I cannot find a medicine to help you."

"My daughter, my spirit is weak. I am ready to go. I will join your mother and your brothers, as well your grandmother and my ancestors. I will die happy, having seen you once again, my daughter."

Sunflower stayed by her father's side until his spirit left him. As Sunflower wept over her father's lifeless body she felt sad but also had a sense of relief and she didn't understand why.

His burial was attended by the few who knew Black Robe as well as Jeremy, Corn Blade and Quiet One. He was buried near the river, his grave adorned with smooth river rocks. Sunflower wished that Reverend Reed could have spoken eloquent words for them and that Melody, with her incredible voice could sing a hymn. As it was, it was quiet with some chanting by Corn Blade.

Two days later they returned to Jeremy's village with Quiet One who willingly came with them. Sunflower introduced her to SnapDragon, who signed to the girl. She looked at Sunflower. Sunflower nodded and Quiet One went with her new teacher.

Little Squirrel was happy to see Sunflower again but when she saw Quiet One with her, she became silent and put on her angry face. Sunflower noticed this and told her about the girl who came with them and how they wanted to help her.

"You can help her too," said Sunflower.

"How can I help? I don't know the silent language," Little Squirrel protested.

"You can help by being a friend to her. Learn the language with her."

Little Squirrel accepted her important duties and even managed a smile.

"Good girl," said Sunflower.

Smiling Face had grown fond of Sunflower and was happy to see her again. She loved SnapDragon and was glad that she and Jeremy would marry but she also wanted Sunflower to become part of her family as well.

When they were alone, Sunflower confided, "When my father died I was sad because after all this time I had finally found him. Yet I was relieved. I don't understand."

Smiling Face reached out her hand to Sunflower. "Jeremy told me your father was ill. I know you did everything in your power to heal him."

"Yes. He was but a shadow of the man I once knew. I didn't recognize him at first. When I told him about my little brothers and the raid on our village, tears fell. He loved us and had been through much. He was sad about Ohum and felt guilty he wasn't there to care for us."

135

Smiling Face gently brushed away a tear from Sunflower's face. "Continue, my daughter."

"During our travels I was sick. I felt weak and sad. I thought I would die, but I didn't. Jeremy helped me during that time and you took such good care of me here. I think that's where I'm confused. I wasn't ready to go, but I know my father was. Is that the difference? He was at peace about it." Sunflower stood. "When Ohum died it was the same. I can't explain it, though."

The older woman said, "I think you've figured it out for yourself. Just as the tree hugs the earth, it will bend in a storm and give up its leaves to the wind. Your father knew it was time to give up his leaves and let go."

"That's it. That is the truth." With a smile, Sunflower continued. "I know you are happy for Jeremy and when I tell you about me, I hope you will be happy for me too." She told Jeremy's mother about Flying Eagle and how she had hesitated to tell Jeremy. "Oh my. I still haven't told him. I must go to him right away."

She hugged Smiling Face. "I love you so much. You are so easy to talk with. In many ways, I feel you're my mother and Ohum rolled into one."

Smiling Face was pleased. "My wish has come true. At last I have the daughter I always desired. I even have called you daughter in my heart."

"You also called me daughter when we were talking just now. That makes me happy too."

Jeremy ambled over to the two women. His mother excused herself, saying she had things to do.

"Is it something I said?" asked Jeremy as his mother stood abruptly.

His mother turned, "No, my son, I really have things to do."

"And I need to talk with you." Sunflower beckoned him.

"Anything at all."

"I told you I was happy that you will take SnapDragon as your wife. I am being truthful. I love her like a sister. I also love you, Jeremy. I love you as a brother and good friend; as you say, *mon ami,* my friend."

He laughed. "I am relieved. I was afraid we'd have too many in the marriage tent. Seriously, I know you like SnapDragon. It means much that you love me too... even if it is as a brother." He pouted.

"Can't you ever be serious?" Sunflower giggled. "Now I can tell you my news. Flying Eagle wants to marry me."

Jeremy's face beamed. "He wants to marry you? Do you want to marry him, my friend?"

"Yes, although my heart is telling me there is something I must do first. I don't know what it is though."

"My dear friend, once when I had a difficult decision to make, my father told me a story about a battle between two wolves. It seems one wolf represents good, which is joy, peace, and love. The other is evil; anger, jealousy, and sorrow. "

"Which wolf won the battle?" asked Sunflower anxiously.

Jeremy laughed. "That's the question I asked my father."

"Well, are you going to tell me what he said?"

"Of course. My father answered simply, 'It is the one you feed.' My dear friend, when the time is right you will know which to feed."

Chapter 18

A Time to Heal

Quiet One learned the new language easily. The change in her was astounding. Whereas she had previously been hunched over, she now stood tall, walked with self-assurance and smiled frequently. Her teacher, SnapDragon, said she wished to teach others so they could communicate with the girl as well.

So together, Jeremy, SnapDragon, Quiet One and even Little Squirrel accompanied Sunflower to present to Chief Bald Eagle a plan to teach the hand language in his village.

The chief mentioned the change in Quiet One. "We may have to change her name," he remarked as he carefully listened to the plan. He suggested that Corn Blade and some of the younger children could be the first students. Then he dismissed the others, asking Sunflower to stay. Little Squirrel was reluctant to leave Sunflower's side but went with Jeremy and the others.

"Young woman, my son has asked my permission to marry you. He said he also asked your father before he died. I have seen how you treated the sick people here in my village," he said. "We have no one here who is knowledgeable in medicine and would like you to be our Village Healer."

Sunflower was stunned. "Thank you. I would like that." She drew in a deep breath. "I am honored but I don't know if I am worthy."

"Let me know your decision soon."

Sunflower felt like she was walking on air. "I know now this is what I must do."

At that moment Flying Eagle rode into the village on his painted horse. Sunflower raced over to him with a big smile on her face. *My, he looks handsome.* He dismounted his horse.

"I need to speak with you," she said.

"Yes, Sunflower, what is it?"

"Remember how I told you there was something I needed to do? I know now what it is. I have been asked to be a Village Healer. I feel certain this is what I must do and I know my grandmother would be most pleased. I think she is smiling down on me even now."

Flying Eagle's face dropped. "My precious love. Does this mean we will not be together? Will you be far from here?"

"You might be happy to know that it is not far from here. In fact, it is here," she said with a twinkle in her eye.

140

"What? Do you mean it? Did my father ask you? I know he was happy with the way you treated our sick people and sewed my niece's finger, but I didn't know he asked you. Did you say, yes?"

"I told him I was honored, but didn't feel worthy. I've prayed to the Great Spirit. If I accept, it would mean that we could marry right away."

"I do want to marry you, the sooner the better."

"Then the decision is made."

"When will you tell my father?" he asked, pulling her close to him.

"I will tell him now. Come with me." Then, pointing, she said with a smile, "Look up at the top of that fir tree. It is the Remembrance Bird."

Everything I say or do
This, Oh Lord, I give to you.
Anything that I can be
This, dear Lord, because of Thee.

CPSIA information can be obtained at www.ICGtesting.com
Printed in the USA
LVOW052305180812

294904LV00003B/14/P